GINSENG AND OTHER TALES FROM MANILA

The publication of this book was supported with grants from the National Endowment for the Arts, the Oregon Arts Commission, and the William A. Gillmore Fund of the Oregon Community Foundation.

Cover art, watercolor/prismacolor by Kristina Kennedy Daniels
Cover and book design
by Darryla Green-McGrath and Cheryl McLean

CALYX Books are distributed to the trade through major library distributors, jobbers, and most small press distributors including: Airlift, Bookpeople, Bookslinger, Inland Book Co., Pacific Pipeline, and Small Press Distribution. For personal orders or other information write: CALYX Books, PO Box B, Corvallis, OR 97339, 503-753-9384.

(∞)

The paper in this book meets the guidelines for permanence and durability of the Committee on Production Guidelines for Book Longevity of the Council on Library Resources and the minimum requirements of the American National Standard for the Permanence of Paper for Printed Library Materials Z38.48-1984.

Library of Congress Cataloging-in-Publication Data

Villanueva, Marianne, 1958-
      Ginseng and other tales from Manila / Marianne Villanueva
         p. cm.
      ISBN 0-934971-20-X (alk.paper):$16.95.—ISBN 0-934971-19-6 (pbk.): $8.95.
        1. Manila (Philippines)—Fiction. I. Title.
  PR9550.9.V49G5 1991
    823—dc20   91-11895
                                     CIP

Printed in the U.S.A.

GINSENG AND OTHER TALES FROM MANILA

Marianne Villanueva

CALYX Books • Corvallis, Oregon

Acknowledgments

The author acknowledges the following publications in which these stories were previously published: "Siko" first appeared in *The Forbidden Stitch: An Asian American Women's Anthology*, CALYX Books, 1989. "Ginseng" previously appeared in *Story Quarterly*, 1987, and in *Panorama*, the Sunday magazine of the *Manila Bulletin*, 1988. "The President's Special Research Project" first appeared in the *Journal of Philippine Studies*, Vol. 33, 1985 as part of *New Writing from the Philippines*.

For Javy and Andrew,
and for my parents

Table of Contents

Preface *ix*

Introduction *xi*

Lizard *1*

Siko *13*

Grandmother *25*

Memorial *29*

Ginseng *39*

The Insult *45*

Overseas *53*

Opportunity *65*

God's Will *73*

The Special Research Project *81*

Island *93*

Glossary *103*

Preface

I began writing again in my mid-twenties, after a period of several years when I did other things—went abroad, dabbled with the idea of being a teacher of Oriental Studies, studied Chinese history.

In the mid-eighties, things were getting very bad in Manila. People were generally of the opinion that the government of Ferdinand Marcos had lost all credibility. On one of my visits home during that time (I was a graduate student at a San Francisco Bay Area college), I noticed how cynical the people seemed. And the stories told to me were stories that, had I not known the people telling them to be absolutely honest and not given to exaggeration, I might have dismissed as being apocryphal. There were stories of the follies of Imelda, who had buildings constructed in three months so structurally unsound one can visit them today, scarcely more than five years later, and see cracks in the cement walls, cracks in the facades, cracks in the ceilings; stories of the Marcos greed; stories of abuses by the military; stories of "salvagings"—the political assassinations that were taking place with disturbing regularity. I saw more beggars on the streets than I had at any time when I was growing up. I heard stories of child prostitutes and of people tortured in detention. All of these stories had a cumulative effect. I felt myself gradually giving in to a rage impossible to put into words. I returned to the San Francisco Bay Area, and a few years later, there was news of the assassination of Benigno Aquino at the Manila International Airport.

I began to write again. I had two years in which to spill out my vitriol, two years granted to me by my enrollment in the Creative Writing Program at Stanford University. I wrote about things people had told me, about stories I read in the newspapers. These stories were so fantastic that I felt the only way to write about them was to emphasize their bizarre nature. Everything I wrote became allegorical. Perhaps I was still afraid of being too direct, of calling a dictator by the names people were calling him in private. Perhaps I felt an allegorical form gave me a measure of distance from the material, a way of shaping it for my artistic purposes. Hence, I began to think of my stories as "tales."

Thus were born stories like "The Special Research Project," "The Insult," and "Memorial." Much to my surprise, the Journal of Philippine studies chose to publish "The Special Research Project" under a slightly different form in 1985, the year before the People Power Revolution occurred, which ended Marcos' twenty-year rule. I felt then that if people were willing to publish such fiction, fiction critical of the dictatorship, albeit masked in allegory, then Marcos had already lost whatever little credibility he thought he had retained. Ensuing events soon bore this out.

Not all of them have to do with the abuses of the Marcos regime. I found myself writing other stories, stories about people I had known, people who were very close to me. And all the time I was writing, it seemed to me that these people's lives were very sad, that they contained elements which troubled me, and that by writing about them I was really exorcising something from my past—my past in a country still suffering from what people call "a colonial mentality"— a country where the "macho" ethic still rules—a polarized country, where the gap between the rich and the poor grows larger every year.

People often say to me: You've lived in America too long. What gives you the right to write about such things? You yourself come from a bourgeois background. How can anyone from a background such as yours write about these things, since you yourself are part of the class system that drags our country down?

To all these people I say: I write because of what I feel. I am a Filipina still, in spite of having lived in America the last ten years. My childhood friends, my family, my teachers—their suffering touches me, and they too deserve a voice. This book is dedicated to them.

Marianne Villanueva

Introduction

Two years ago, on one of those cool San Francisco evenings, I had the privilege of participating in a book party/reading for *The Forbidden Stitch* anthology. The most memorable moment of that evening for me was the opportunity to meet and hear from Marianne Villanueva. I was impressed by her short story "Siko" in the CALYX publication, and the opportunity to meet a good, finely crafted practicing Filipina or Filipina American woman writer is a rare find.

I was not disappointed. From the mind and heart of this delicate Filipina emerged the most enchanting tales and the most intriguing stories. That is why I was so pleased to be asked to write this introduction for her collection, *Ginseng and Other Tales from Manila*.

I have read every tale in this collection. After each reading, I shook my head in admiration for her craft as a storyteller and in wonder for her ability to so carefully weave a story and characters that capture the Filipino sensibility between reality and myth, between the tangibility of the New West and the intangible beliefs of the Filipino.

Villanueva's writing straddles the netherworld between early Filipino history, Philippine folktales/myth, present day newspaper headlines, and *chismis*, that fine art of Filipino gossip. *Chismis*, artfully executed, can begin to topple governments earlier than the stock market, and can certainly fuel any revolution.

To read a Villanueva tale is to enter this world. It is seeing the slow demise of a Philippine dictator through the eyes of his ghostwriter. It is walking in the feet of a young barrio girl as she puzzles through the poverty of her life, unwittingly abandoned by a beloved brother gone to work overseas. It is to live with *bahala na*—leaving to the forces of fate the tabloid rise and fall of a B-grade Philippine movie star. It is to know the heart-wrenching struggle of Philippine intelligentsia, as a professor through desperation, cunning, and creativity finds an outlet to state his rejection of the cruelty and lawlessness of modern Philippine society.

But Marianne's stories are not violent. Rather, they are tales of survival and those talismans that have made these Filipino characters survivors and, perhaps, even everyday heroes in a world of tragedy.

Villanueva's strength is her ability to carefully draw mood and setting—whether modern Manila or the timelessness of the countryside, her narrative skill and use of characterization to bring the reader into a Filipino character's point of view, and her subtle use of plot to capture the reader until the tale's end.

With this collection, Villanueva steps onto the level of writers like N.V.M. Gonzales, Bienvenido Santos, and Linda Ty-Casper. And the frightening and exhilarating discovery is that these stories are just the first touchstone in what promises to be a literary career of many more intriguing tales to come.

Virginia R. Cerenio
San Francisco, California
February 18, 1991

Lizard

When Wito was little, strangers had a way of coming up to her and saying, "I knew your mother when you were not even a twinkle in her eye." Then they would tell her stories of how, when her mother was only thirteen or fourteen, they had seen her in a concert, or how they had taken the ferry with her once from Bacolod to Iloilo. Sometimes, returning home from school in the late afternoon, Wito would see a stranger sitting on the *lanai* with her mother, having a late afternoon meal. At her entrance, the stranger would look startled and say something like, "Is this—? I had no idea how big she was! How long has it been since—?"

Listening to all these strangers, Wito learned that her mother had been quite famous—that once she had played the piano and traveled from town to town, giving concerts. Her mother didn't seem to want to talk about those days, though other people reminded her. Then she would tell Wito that she had led a very hard life, and that she got paid very little for her concerts, perhaps only a few dozen *pesos* for hours of practice, that often she played for people who didn't understand the music and talked and ate while she played. She said she did it only because she was poor, and because her own mother needed things like a refrigerator, a stove. She said she never saw any of the money she made; she gave it all to her mother.

As Wito's mother talked, Wito would watch her face—the large, dark eyes growing alternately bitter and sad. Her mother was very dark. Growing up, she said, the neighborhood children called her *balut*—duckling egg. Wito's grandmother tried all sorts of things to make her more *mestiza*—rubbing *kalamansi* juice on her skin twice a day, applying a paste made from menstrual blood—but none of it seemed to work.

Because she had been playing the piano since she was four, her hands were not like those of the other girls—the palms were hard and stiff, and large blue veins leaped out between the bones. She kept them folded up in her skirt, or resting, palms upward, on her lap. After many years, it began to hurt to straighten the fingers, and so she kept them curled up all the time, like the fingers of a paralytic.

Whenever Wito heard her mother speak, and looked at her twisted hands, she felt very sorry for her. She herself was always so full of complaints. She hated, for instance, to eat okra, which the cook served nearly every day because it was her father's favorite vegetable, and she hated the nuns at the convent school, who were always scolding her for talking too loudly or for not sitting with her knees together. But what were all these difficulties in comparison to being made to sit at the piano for four hours straight, playing the same piece over and over, as her grandmother had made her mother do?

When Wito was the new girl at school, the nuns were very excited and were always asking her to play something. Wito knew only "chopsticks" and some tunes she could play by ear. When it finally came out that she could not play, Mother Remedios, the music teacher, could not conceal her disappointment. "What a shame!" she said. "What a shame!" Wito had to squeeze her hands hard between her knees to keep from saying something. If anyone had asked her for an explanation, she would have said that there was a piano in their home, which stood in a corner of the living room. It was not at all like the piano at school, which was small and badly scratched, and where Mother Remedios sat day after day banging out "Assumpta est Maria" for the congregation. The piano at home was black and enormous, a Steinway, the only one of its kind in the town. Every day a maid ran a soft cloth over the yellowing ivory keys, and now and then Wito would see a man come to strike the chords and, listening, nod his head, like a doctor satisfied with a patient's heartbeat. But whereas the piano at school was homely and seemed expressly made for Mother Remedios's flailing attacks on it, the piano at home had at some point, and Wito could not explain how, acquired an aura of evil, so that its being in the house at all came to seem like something of a curse. Wito knew very well that her mother cared nothing for it and would have had it taken away if not for the protests of her grandmother.

Because there were always others in school who behaved like Mother Remedios and assumed Wito was musically accomplished, Wito learned that there were certain things people expected of her mother and, by extension, of herself. These people would loom before her, smiling and loud, and say, "Play something for us! Play!" But when they discovered Wito could not play, they would become very disappointed, and then they would turn their backs and forget about her.

Wito had seen the pictures of her mother in the photo albums: the black and white pictures of her mother dressed in flowing gowns, holding bouquets of roses, and smiling at the camera. In the pictures her mother's face was very round, and her eyebrows very dark and pointed, and she smiled as though she were afraid of something. But the dresses hanging in Wito's mother's closet now were different. They were ordinary dresses for going to the market or for visiting with relatives.

Sometimes, late at night, Wito would be awakened by an unfamiliar sound. She would lie on her back, staring at the big grey lizard who lived on her ceiling. Sometimes she thought she could make out the lizard's heartbeat in its throat, which went up and down, up and down, in time to some music. It always took her some time to realize that the music was coming from downstairs, from the piano. The sound was wild and sorrowful, and Wito did not like listening to it. She would put her pillows over her ears, and curl up tightly in her blanket, trying to shut out the noise. It always seemed a long, long time before the sound stopped and she could fall asleep again. That was how Wito came to think of the piano and the night as belonging together.

But these were not things she could tell anyone in her school, not even her best friend Veronica, who lived just around the corner and who often came over to play. Veronica's mother had said to Wito once: "I read something about your mother in the *Manila Chronicle*. Is she still playing?" Wito could only shake her head dumbly. Veronica's mother had gone on to say what a shame that was; Wito's mother had been a famous pianist before she had gotten married.

Wito's grandmother had said once that Wito's hands were like her mother's. She could never forget that day. Wito had been digging for earthworms in the garden, not for any particular reason but because it was something she liked to do, when her grandmother came up unexpectedly behind her and said, "You have your mother's hands." At that time, it had frightened Wito very much. She hadn't known what it meant, to have such hands. Only it seemed to her that her mother was often sad, and that perhaps if her hands were not that way she would be happier. At first, looking at her hands, Wito saw only that they were white and smooth. She could not see anything in them that even closely resembled her mother's. After a while she thought she could just make out the faint, blue tracery of veins beneath the skin, and at one point in particular, just between her right thumb and forefinger, the vein was unusually prominent. When she wrote something, the vein bulged with the effort, and sometimes it writhed and even seemed to jump. Then Wito worried very much, and tried massaging that particular place or letting her hand dangle in cold running water until she saw the vein begin to subside a little.

Whenever her grandmother visited, Wito remained up in her room. Everything about the old woman seemed hard—the way her cheek felt when Wito greeted her, the way she held her back when she was supposed to be reclining on the sofa. Even her hair was hard and springy. It rose straight up from her forehead with two white streaks on either side, making her look, to Wito, like a witch. Her eyes were small—two bright black points—and her lips were thin and always tightly pressed together.

Wito noticed that her grandmother came more often during the milling season, when Wito's father had to stay late on the farm. At such times, her grandmother would spend nearly an entire day at the house. She would be at the breakfast table when Wito came down in the morning, and she would still be there at dinnertime, sitting in her father's accustomed place, helping herself to the dishes the maid passed around the table.

Then her grandmother would take it into her head that Wito must learn how to play the piano. Her hard fingers on Wito's shoulder would propel the girl to the piano stool, and sitting there, Wito would be forced to look at the piano pieces her grandmother had brought with her—pieces that seemed like ciphers, with odd little symbols that Wito could never understand, no matter how often her grandmother explained them. Her grandmother would sigh, and in that sigh was some deep and buried anger Wito could feel. It frightened her. Her grandmother would take Wito's fingers and spread them open over the keys. "This way, this way," she would say.

The summer Wito was eight, there was a drought and her father was often away for days at a time. He was worried about the farm, and about whether the *sakadas* were getting enough water for themselves.

Wito expected her grandmother to come over more often, but for a long time she stayed away. Finally, when she did come, she seemed to bring with her a great bitterness. Wito saw her one day when she had just come home from school, sitting with her mother on the flowered sofa on the *lanai*.

They must have been sitting there a long time. Her grandmother was leaning forward, saying something in a low insistent voice, while Wito's mother listened with bent head. Wito saw how intently her grandmother gazed at her mother, how there seemed to be something about her mother that kept drawing the older woman forward, so that it seemed she might reach out any moment and touch or, perhaps, hit her. Wito saw how her mother hung her head, and knew that she was crying. The back of her neck, covered with fine, black hair, looked narrow and exposed. Wito thought she caught the words "shameful" and "waste," but then her grandmother saw her and broke off abruptly.

When Wito went up to greet her grandmother, the old woman's cheek felt dry, like parchment, whereas her mother's cheek was soft and moist, and when Wito turned to leave, her mother softly said "no" and pulled her close. Her mother's arms encircled her, forcing her to face her grandmother. The old woman looked down at Wito, and in her eyes there was nothing of love or sympathy, or even recognition.

Her mother remained holding Wito like that for a long time, not looking again at Wito's grandmother. Finally the old woman said, "Pah!" impatiently and got up to go. She walked slowly and stiffly down the length of the *lanai*, and Wito could hear her jabbing angrily with her cane at the plants in the garden. It seemed a long time before she heard the gate shut.

That night Wito's mother was very quiet. When Wito went to her to ask to be held, she said, "Not now, it is time for your bath," and when Wito came back a little later, "I am tired. See what Zenaida is cooking for supper." Wito's father returned earlier than expected, and Wito saw her mother sigh, as though her father's coming only added to her trouble.

Wito's father had just come from the farm, yet his white shoes were immaculate. His polished fingernails gleamed in the light of the dining room chandelier.

Wito's mother had told her that when Wito's father was growing up, he had a boy follow after him to tie his shoelaces whenever they came undone. This boy, an old man now, still came around now and then and told Wito's mother stories of when her husband was a young boy, and how he had rescued him from this and that scrape. Wito, too, would listen, and it seemed to her that her father and her mother's childhoods were very different, and that the difference was so great it seemed a miracle her father and her mother had ever found each other.

Wito's mother asked all the usual questions—how the *enkargados* were getting along, whether Pacing, the wife of one of the *sakadas*, had her baby yet, and whether much damage had been inflicted by the drought. Her father answered distractedly. The cook served cabbage rolls, fish stew, and the inevitable okra. Her father ate with great appetite, hunched over his plate.

As he ate, Wito found herself looking carefully at her father's face. Before, she had considered him ugly. Her father had a large, squashed-looking nose that was somehow always red, and he had the square face and heavy jowls of a bulldog. His hair began halfway back from his head, and there was not much of it. Moreover, it was always greasy and smelled of a pungent, green gel that Wito's mother called *"pomada."*

Wito knew almost everything that had happened between her father and her mother before she was born. Her mother liked to say how her father had camped out on her doorstep for days, and although she didn't like him at first, she finally began to pity him. Wito's grandmother had been against her father. She had made disparaging remarks about him whenever he came to visit. Wito's mother said she began to love Wito's father because of the patient way he would sit in the living room, waiting for her and pretending not to hear the harangues of Wito's grandmother. When things became very bad between Wito's mother and her grandmother, her parents eloped. Her mother left her family a note, explaining what she had done and why, and asked them to please keep all her concert gowns because she didn't want to see them any longer. Wito's grandmother had been so angry that even after Wito was born, it was some months before she could bring herself to visit her daughter's house. Then, when she finally did have a look at Wito, she noted that the baby had her father's small, wide-set eyes, and pronounced her ugly. Wito's mother had immediately snatched her up and fled from the room, but it was too late. Some of her grandmother's sentiment had already been communicated to Wito. That was why she was always ashamed when visitors to the house would look at her and say, "She takes after her father." After that, she would stick a clothespin on her nose when she thought no one was looking.

Her father was always silent. Her mother was usually gay and full of stories, while her father sat stolidly behind his newspaper, and did not seem interested in the things Wito had to tell him. The only time he held her was when she kissed him goodnight. Wito was afraid that if her father found out what she thought of his looks, he would be very angry. He might even begin to dislike her.

But this evening, it seemed that her father's arrival dispelled the bad feeling her grandmother had left in the house. This bad feeling had seemed to hover over everything, so that she took no pleasure in playing in the garden as she usually did in the late afternoon, nor even in the bowl of yams boiled in coconut milk that Zenaida had made especially for her. Now that her father was home, everything was all right once more. She was glad to watch him eat, glad to watch him enjoying his food. For this reason, she could not understand why her mother said suddenly, in the middle of the meal, "*Mamang* was here today."

After speaking, a stubborn look came over her mother's face, and it seemed she didn't want to talk anymore. Wito's father continued sucking on a fish bone for a few moments. Then, without raising his head, he said quietly, "What did she want?"

"Oh!" her mother said, making a gesture of exasperation. "She was in one of her moods again. She went on and on about how I was wasting my talent, that I should start giving concerts again. I told her I wasn't interested in that kind of life any longer, and it led to her saying other things. She was angry, so angry!"

Her mother went on in this vein for a few more moments. Her

father only grunted now and then in reply, while scooping some last bits of rice into his mouth. After a while he noticed Wito staring and said, "If you've finished eating, you can leave the table."

Wito got up at once. Almost as soon as she stepped out of the dining room, she heard her mother's voice resume its complaints. The sound was like a river, the way it flowed and twisted about, but always rushing, rushing forward, and her father's occasional grunts were like the rocks that stood in that river, stoic and indifferent. Wito herself could not withstand the force of this river. It was so hard, so petulant, so full of bitterness and suffering. She went up to her room, feeling tired and a little sad.

When Zenaida came up as usual to undress Wito and put her to bed, she found her already curled up in her blanket, her head buried in her pillow.

"What's the matter?" Zenaida asked. "Aren't you feeling well?"

Wito shook her head.

Zenaida had been her *yaya* since Wito was a baby. The woman used to sleep on a mat at the foot of Wito's bed, but just this year her father had ordered Zenaida to sleep downstairs with the other help, saying that Wito was "getting too big for that." Wito had not complained before, but now she wanted her *yaya* to stay and put her arms around her.

Zenaida knelt by the bed and felt Wito's forehead. Her hands felt cool, the roughened palms strangely comforting. Wito looked up at the woman's face. It was a homely face, broad and flat with small, black eyes set close together on either side of a bridgeless nose. There was a scar running from the bottom of her nose through her upper lip that, Wito's mother had explained once, had been the result of an operation. Because of this disfigurement, Wito had never thought of Zenaida as being the same as other people. She had often made fun of her behind her back, and imitated her slow, stolid walk. But now, looking at that face, she did not find it ugly. She remained looking at Zenaida for a long time, until she fell asleep.

The next day was Saturday. Since there was no school, Wito could stay in bed late. She lay on her stomach, listening to her own breathing, to the bird sounds in the garden. As she tried to recall the events of the previous evening, she was overcome by a form of nausea, strange and unexplained. It made her feel as though she were standing on the rolling deck of a great ship. She remembered Zenaida coming in, and Zenaida's cool hand pressed against her forehead, and she remembered watching to see if Zenaida would pull her hand away in fright because Wito felt sure that she was indeed very, very hot inside. But Zenaida had said only, "It is nothing" and then turned off the light—wasn't that what she had done?—and then for a long time Wito had remained awake in the darkness, trying to puzzle out the meaning of her mother's bitterness.

It seemed to her that in one way or another, in all her parents' conversations, they always came up against this "thing," like an obstacle that one is careful to walk around. It was shadowy now, but sometimes, like last night, it would assume unexpected shape and significance. It would emerge, startling and huge, as out of a mist, and then even ordinary, everyday things—this cup Wito was holding in her hand, the saucer for it to rest on, this bowl with the chipped edge, this slant of light, this leaf, oh, everything!—became twisted out of shape, not themselves. Perhaps this explained the nausea that Wito felt whenever the horizon, which should stay still, would not. She had felt it standing on the deck of the great ship (which was in actuality only the ferry; she had taken it dozens of times, back and forth between the islands). At that time the clouds had looked like whorls—spinning, spinning.

Perhaps this was why Wito could not bear to see her mother crying or looking even a little sad. When she saw her mother was in one of her moods, she would sing and dance and clap her hands, as though the sound of her voice and her clapping were all the cure her mother needed. She would pat her mother's hair, her arms, her lips, in a sudden excess of anxiety, as though her mother were a thing in danger of breaking apart like the eggs Zenaida cracked in the kitchen, and only the pressure of Wito's hands could hold all the pieces together.

Now she heard her mother's voice below, speaking to the gardener. It was a cheerful, even voice, not the one of last night. It was nearly noon. The trees at the far edge of the garden looked strangely flat—like paper cutouts. Her mother, in a bright pink sundress, a golf umbrella balanced over her right shoulder to shield her from the sun, was bending over some bushes. When she moved, she seemed to blur a little.

Wito lay back on her bed and closed her eyes. Through her eyelids she could feel the sun in hot pulses of light. Was she only imagining it or had she really seen the *gumamela*, the *santan*, all in bloom at once, all along the garden wall? Even now that she had her eyes closed and was lying back on the bed, she could still see the reds and oranges of the flowers seeming to blaze among the cool green of the leaves. She imagined she could smell the newly cut grass and the fresh-dug earth where her mother was getting ready to plant a new tree. A strange thought came to her: perhaps, if she went to the garden at this moment, she would find her mother as she had been, restored and whole. Then she would will her to remain that way forever. The longing to see her mother whole again became so overwhelming that Wito immediately got up and dressed.

Once outside, Wito paused. The heat was intense. It clung to her face and arms, to the back of her neck. The grass was dry—so dry it seemed to have bleached out and faded. The earth was hard and packed, and Wito thought how, even if it were to rain now, there could not be much water that could penetrate that sealed surface.

She saw her mother leaning against a corner of the house, waving a palm-leaf fan slowly back and forth across her face. Her mother had not seen her. She was looking down at the ground and seemed to be thinking. Just at the moment when Wito would have called out to her, she caught sight of something reflected against the white wall of the house. An unexpected shadow had appeared in profile to her mother's body. There was a head, or what Wito assumed was a head, though it looked nothing like her mother's, and had long, pointed teeth. When her mother turned her head a little, the shadow moved, too. Only when Wito had come a little closer did she finally make out what it was—there, growing out of her mother's back, was a huge, scaly lizard.

Wito did not scream, did not cry out. Even when the thing actually raised its head and looked straight at her, she did not think to run away. She saw how her mother continued to walk by the wall, bending down every now and then to inspect the flower beds, and how easily she carried the creature on her back, as though it had no weight at all. When her mother straightened abruptly, the creature did not fall, did not even slip, but remained looking blandly at Wito over her mother's shoulder, its long red tongue just brushing her mother's right ear. When her mother raised a hand to tuck a loose strand of hair behind her ear, the creature adroitly moved its head to avoid touching her.

Just then her mother saw Wito and smiled. When she smiled, her cheeks jumped up, nearly covering her eyes. Her hair was in a bun at the back of her head, but a few strands had escaped near the bottom and clung in little damp circles to her neck. Her neck, Wito noticed for the first time, was thick, with little grooves running all around it.

"Come, Wito!" her mother called. "Shall we have breakfast?"

Wito merely nodded and trailed slowly behind her mother, from a distance.

Her father was reclining on the sofa on the *lanai*, reading the paper. When her mother called to him, he quickly put down his paper and joined them at the dining room table. Wito saw that he was preoccupied. He hardly touched the mangoes, dried fish, and fried sweet sausage that her mother placed before him. After a long silence he said, "I must get back to the farm. There's a lot of work to be done."

Her mother made no comment but calmly continued passing the dishes and pouring the coffee. "Would you like some of this, Wito?" she would ask from time to time, and took no notice when Wito failed to answer her. Finally she turned to her husband and said, "When will you be back?"

"Late," Wito's father replied. "We have to find more spring water— there's no telling how much longer this drought will last."

Wito kept looking at her father, but he was eating just the way he always did: hunched over his plate, fingers holding a dried fish to his mouth. He didn't seem to notice anything different about his wife. But then, Wito thought, perhaps he had grown used to the thing growing out of her back, and no longer thought about it.

Wito wondered how it was when her mother slept. Did she sleep peacefully or did the thing torment her, making it difficult, for example, for her to lie on her back or to breathe properly? She wondered if her father, reaching for her mother in the middle of the night, did not brush against the thing by accident, and think perhaps it was his wife's face that he had touched.

When the maid came to clear away the dishes, Wito's mother went back into the garden, but Wito excused herself and went up to her room. There, she ran to the window and looked at her mother in the garden. From this distance, she couldn't make out the creature, and her mother was just a woman in a pink sundress bending over a bougainvillea bush.

Now it seemed to Wito that the mother she had known was

another person, different from this one who had just been revealed. When Wito thought of that mother now, it was as though she existed only in the past, as though all the things they had done together were remembered, like pictures in an album. She began to go over some of their favorite activities in her mind. In the evening, her mother had sometimes called Wito to come and brush her hair. Then, handing Wito the ivory-handled brush, she would sit on a low stool in front of her, with her back turned. Wito remembered how heavy her mother's long, black hair had felt in her hands, how difficult it had always been to brush, like brushing the matted fur of some animal, and how it always smelled faintly of coconut oil. Her mother would turn her head now and then to look at Wito and smile, and in smiling looked so beautiful that Wito was reminded of the statue of the Virgin in the Santuario de San Antonio.

Then there had been the times at the farm when Wito had watched her mother talking to the *sakadas*. How they had looked at her, those people without any shoes—with shining, grateful eyes, as though she were a Maria Makiling just come down from the mountain. "Ah, Impeng," her mother would say to one, "you seem to have lost your teeth," and the poor soul could only giggle in sudden embarrassment, covering her toothless mouth with one hand.

At other times, her mother asked her to sit on her lap and they would play silly games. Her favorite was the one where her mother would ask, "Who is my *kamatis*? Who is my *sibuyas*?" How happy it made her to shout "me" to each of her mother's questions, and to be rewarded with one of her mother's kisses.

At such times, she could almost believe that her mother was another person, a person who laughed and whose laugh had truth and substance, whose laugh chased away poisons and evil spirits and made things whole when they were broken. This mother, Wito could easily believe, lived in light and air, and moved about easily in brightly lit rooms, singing.

Now Wito heard her father's voice in the garden, and she ran to the window to see him. Her father was taking his leave of her mother. He turned to go but something her mother said made him turn, made him come back and rest a large, clumsy hand on the back of her neck. Wito's mother bent her head, and the shadow on the grass opened its mouth and showed its long, pointed teeth.

Siko

The village of Bagong Silang is an untidy assortment of half a dozen palm-thatched houses, about a hundred kilometers north of Manila. It falls under the jurisdiction of the municipality of San Pablo, a town of a few hundred people, a day's walk away. The people of Bagong Silang have lived for generations along a narrow strip of mud road that borders the rice paddies. They are, as a rule, thrifty and industrious folk. When not toiling in the rice fields, they tend vegetable gardens. They own a few pigs, a few chickens—nothing much else of value.

Aling Saturnina used to live in the last house on the left, the one behind the *santol* tree. But last year, she and her married daughter were taken to San Pablo in a military jeep, and since then no one has seen or heard from them. The villagers don't like to talk about the events that led to *Aling* Saturnina's disappearance. When asked, they cross themselves and their eyes slide sideways and perhaps one or two will invoke the name of the town's patron saint, as though the saying of it had the power to protect them from all harm. If the questioner becomes too persistent— as lately some of these newspapermen from San Pablo have been— they escape to the rice fields, and wait there till nightfall before returning to their homes. They are simple folk and don't bother with things they cannot understand.

Everyone remembers *Aling* Saturnina because of her temper. She had eight children, and was always cursing and beating one or the other with the back of her wooden slippers. She was fond of *tuba*, the potent drink made from fermented palm sap. Whether or not she had money for the children's supper, she would send one of her sons to the *tiyanggi* for a bottle. The eldest son, Lando, ran away when he was fourteen. A few years later, Isagani left. Then, in quick succession, Prospero, Lina, Catherine, and Rey, too, disappeared.

Siko stayed until he was nearly full-grown. When he finally left, he took the last of his mother's savings with him— a few crumpled *pesos,* which she had kept in a tin tucked away under the eaves of the house. When *Aling* Saturnina discovered the loss, her curses could be heard all over the village. Now there was no money for *tuba,* and the youngest child, Ana, was a skinny, sickly girl, not much use out in the rice fields. The villagers avoided *Aling* Saturnina then because she would pace the street restlessly with feverish, yellow eyes, like a bitch in heat. They felt sorry for Ana, but what could they do? Sometimes they would press a few eggs into her hands, a few clumps of spinach. No one was surprised when, soon after Siko's departure, Ana took Poldo as a husband. There was no money for a church wedding, so Poldo simply moved in. Poldo proved to be a good son-in-law, a hard worker. He and Ana lived peacefully together in *Aling* Saturnina's house for many years.

One day, *Aling* Saturnina learned that Siko had been killed. It was Ana who brought her the news, Ana who came stumbling down the narrow street, crying and blowing her nose into her skirt. At first, *Aling* Saturnina was confused. Hands knotting her dress in anxiety, she ordered Ana to compose herself.

"Ah, *Ina!*" Ana cried. "Siko has been shot! He was caught breaking into a colonel's house in San Pablo."

Aling Saturnina sighed. She was not sad, no. She had not seen him in such a long time, and sometimes it pleased her to think that she could no longer remember his face, not even when, in those moments when she was without *tuba,* she wrinkled her forehead and tried hard to concentrate. He had hurt her, how he had hurt her! The memory of that bitter day when, with trembling fingers, she had reached up to the roof and lifted down the old tin can where she had ten, perhaps fifteen *pesos* lovingly stored, and prying open the lid with her anxious fingers, had seen only emptiness staring back at her—ah! That memory rushed over her once again with overwhelming clarity. She remembered the helpless feeling—as though she had been hit in the belly—that had accompanied her discovery. She had no *tuba* all that day, or the next, and her body had been wracked by chills, she had been in a fever of want. Over and over again, on those sleepless nights when she found herself pacing the village like a restless animal, she asked herself, "How could he do this to me?" She thought, for a time, that of all her children, Siko loved her the most. She had kept him warm beside her on cold nights. She had taken care never to beat him—not even when he had done something that angered her—preferring instead to beat Lando, because Lando was the eldest and should have been responsible for the behavior of his younger brothers and sisters. She had never suspected Siko of stealing, though after he had gone she began to hear stories from the neighbors, stories of how he had been caught more than once filching tomatoes from their vegetable gardens, and how when baby chickens disappeared, they all thought instinctively of Siko. How was it that she had never known? A son of hers a thief! *Aling* Saturnina was ashamed. And now this horrifying deed—breaking into someone's home, and that someone no less than a colonel! It was beyond *Aling* Saturnina's comprehension. She should have known, she berated herself, she should have known all along. Her heart was thudding painfully. The ingrate! She wanted to curse, to beat the air with her fists.

She looked at Ana crying helplessly in a corner.

"That's enough!" she cried. "You'll make yourself sick. Your brother was a fool, may lightning strike me, but he was. I would have beaten any of you with my *tsinelas* if I had caught you stealing so much as a twig from a neighbor's garden!"

Then she went to the shelf where she kept a bottle of *tuba*, and took it with her to the rice fields.

As her feet trod the worn paths threading the rice paddies, *Aling* Saturnina's spirit remained cold and unforgiving. Her mind gnawed ceaselessly at the fact of Siko's betrayal. That fact had assumed the hardness and blackness of a kernel, lodged at the front of her forehead, between her eyes. On this she focused all her attention. She was oblivious to the fresh green of the rice saplings that blanketed the wet earth, the brilliant blue arch of the sky, the birds gliding soundlessly overhead. The silence wrapped itself around her like a cloak. The village dropped farther and farther behind until it was no more than an indistinct blur on the horizon.

Aling Saturnina grew tired. She decided to sit and rest for a while in one of the bamboo thickets that sprouted up here and there, forming pockets of dry land among the paddies. As she stretched out on the hard, packed earth and looked around her, her eyes beheld the great, blue bulk of The Mountain, rising straight up out of the plain. The Mountain made her think contemptuously of the legend the villagers told their young children, the legend of the enchantress, Maria Cacao, who was said to live in a palace of gold on The Mountain's highest peak. Now and then, the villagers said, she ventured down to the lowlands and lured men away from their homes and families. *Aling* Saturnina had stopped believing this story a long time ago. She knew now that when sons and husbands disappeared from the village, as her own had done, they had been lured away by more dangerous enchantments, such as were to be found in the big city of Manila, not far to the south. Her husband had left her after one such trip to the city, never to return. And the rest of her sons, the ones who were still living—they were probably there too, living in the shantytown of Tondo, which she had heard was twice as large as the municipality of San Pablo. Some day, *Aling* Saturnina thought, some day I'll go after those bastards.

She sat in the fields, letting the wind riffle through her long, gray hair and calm her aching nerves. Now and then she took deep, long gulps of the *tuba*. She sat there a long time, until it grew dark and the rice paddies, filled with water, began to reflect the light of the moon. A cold wind rose and parted the bamboo thickets. Still she sat and stared. After a while, she thought she could hear a great clamor of barking dogs arising from the village, and she rose, suddenly expectant. She looked toward the village, ears straining. The clamor increased in ferocity. She could imagine the village dogs, twisting and straining on their hind legs, jaws agape. She had seen them bark in unison like this many other times, and always, always, the sleepy villagers, rushing to their windows in the dead of night, had seen, coming down the street, strange, pale figures—ghosts, spirits, goblins. The last time, they had seen the ghost of *Aling* Corazon's daughter. She had drowned herself in the Agno River after her husband left her. Her ghost had walked slowly down the middle of the street, crying silently and wringing her hands. At intervals she would stop and look around with imploring eyes. The villagers had watched *Aling* Corazon, to see what she would do, but she remained dry-eyed at her window, and, after the wraith had passed, she closed her shutters and went to bed, like all the rest.

In a little while, *Aling* Saturnina thought she could hear Siko's voice, breaking through a gust of wind. The clumps of bamboo trembled and swayed. *Aling* Saturnina wondered what form her son would take in coming to her. Would he come as a huge black dog or a pig? She had heard that spirits liked to assume such disguises. Would he appear as one of those bat-like creatures that fly through the air with only the upper halves of their bodies? Several of the villagers had sworn they had seen such things hovering over the rice fields.

Just then, something dark dropped from the sky and landed before her with a soft thud. *Aling* Saturnina saw that it was a man squatting on his haunches, head lowered, palms pressed against the earth. He raised his head, revealing a blood-spattered face. It was Siko.

Even with his face so disfigured by blood, there was no mistaking the gap between his two front teeth, almost exactly like the one her husband had. Siko squatted, grinning, in the moonlight. He was wearing blue jeans and a white cotton T-shirt, and there were dark, purplish patches of clotted blood across his chest. After she recovered from her initial surprise, *Aling* Saturnina wanted to hit him. But what was the use of hitting a ghost? Instead she cried: "*Walang hiya ka*! How dare you take my money, leave me and your sister to starve to death!"

As soon as she said those words, she felt her limbs stiffen and become curiously immobile. She wanted to cry out but her tongue lay leaden in her mouth. She could not even reach for the bottle of *tuba* at her feet. Siko stopped grinning. He stood up and approached her, scrutinizing her face. He came so close that she could distinctly smell the odor from his rotting gums.

"*Kumusta ka, Ina?*" he said in a teasing tone of voice, a tone he might have used if he had seen her once a week all his life. "I am very pleased to see you again. It's good to see you looking so well."

He laughed soundlessly and *Aling* Saturnina shuddered. She wondered if he had returned to do her harm. She had nothing to defend herself with, not even one of those pictures of the Holy Family which the other old women of the village wore on cords around their necks, not even a bit of ginger pinned to her dress.

"Don't be alarmed, *Ina*," Siko continued. "I've forgiven you everything, even for the fact that you seemed to care more about the *tuba* than any of your children. Perhaps you couldn't help it. No one wants to be poor—mud between your toes all your life, *nipa* hut blown down with every typhoon. What a life!"

You bastard, *Aling* Saturnina thought. Who told you to go and kill that man?

"Let me tell you about that man," Siko went on. "He was rich. You know how it is. After years in the army you become a *padrón*. People come to you for special favors, and of course you would not be so stupid as to help without getting anything in return. It's why everyone wants to enter the army in the first place. Take any poor boy from the provinces, give him 20 years in the army, and at the end of that time he ought to have enough to retire comfortably in a mansion—two, if he's any kind of operator."

But you did not have to kill him, *Aling* Saturnina thought.

It became quiet—so quiet that *Aling* Saturnina could hear the dogs of the village barking again. Far off she could make out one or two lights against the darkness of the rice paddies. There were a few people awake, but they would not venture outside on a night like this, not with the dogs warning them away.

Siko was squatting on the ground again, staring morosely at his wounds. He seemed to be remembering something. When he spoke again his voice was sad:

"You remember *Ate* Lina? Little, snot-nosed Lina who was always falling into a pile of *carabao* dung when she was young?"

Ah, *Aling* Saturnina thought. Lina.

"You're frowning," Siko continued. "You look uncertain. Perhaps you don't remember? No matter. She'd changed her name so many times. At one time she was 'Fleur-de-lis,' a waitress at the Fishnet in Manila. Later, when she became a taxi dancer, she changed her name to 'Pepsi.' Pepsi Perez. When I met her again last year, she was working the bars in Olongapo. She had gone back to using her own name because it didn't seem to matter to her anymore what she did. She had a regular customer, this colonel. 'In a little while,' she told me, 'this life will be over for me. I'll be a straight woman.'"

No, *Aling* Saturnina thought. No, that doesn't sound like Lina.

"Let me tell you, let me tell you, *Ina*." Siko said. "The colonel was not the first man I killed. There was another one in Aliaga. But he was only a minor official with the Bureau of Land Transportation. After a few days, the case was closed. His wife and two children lived way out in Cagayan de Oro. What could they do? No one worth anything comes from Cagayan de Oro."

Ah, how evil! *Aling* Saturnina thought.

"I admit that I felt sorry about that man afterward," Siko went on. "He was only doing his duty and not even getting rich by it. But this lousy colonel..."

Siko paused. His face became momentarily indistinct. Then he said, "I'll tell you how it was. This colonel was a dog, a real dog. I don't know what gutter he crawled out from. I could have killed him when I first saw him touch my sister. But Lina begged me not to. She said she had a plan, that I should be patient. 'One day,' she said, 'we'll come into our own.'"

"So I waited. I was patient. Lina became the colonel's mistress. He took her up with him to San Pablo and I did not even try to follow. Now and then, I heard things. I heard that this colonel had a wife, a real shrew. She was used to her husband bringing home girls and she was not fooled when the colonel introduced Lina as his masseuse. Later I heard that she had threatened to go after Lina with a knife. Things were getting bad for Lina but every time I wanted to go and get her she said, 'Wait.' Well, the day came when she said, 'Come.' And when I saw her she had a broken nose and bruises all over her chest and back. The colonel had gotten tired of her and stood by while his wife did this. Lina was crying and saying, 'Let's get out of here.' I said, 'Not before getting what's our due.' So that night I went up to the colonel's house. It was a mansion right at the edge of town, with tennis courts in the back and a swimming pool a mile long. You see how these dogs live!

"I had just gotten over the garden wall when—bang!—I heard a shot and part of my right ear flew off. A fat woman with hair all done up in curlers was standing a little way off. I guessed she must be the colonel's wife. She was very angry. 'Get him, you fool!' she kept shouting. I turned and saw the colonel behind me, preparing to shoot again. But he was having trouble—his gun had jammed. I started laughing then, because he was cowering in front of me like a frightened rat. I took his gun and cracked his skull with it. The next thing I knew, I was lying on the ground, and the last thing I saw before the world went black was the ugly face of the colonel's wife, leering over me with a knife."

Siko stopped, took a deep breath, and shuddered. *Aling* Saturnina moaned and closed her eyes. She was crying. She had not cried for years—not even when her husband left her, not even when her parents died, not even when, right after Siko left, the days of going without *tuba* left her weak and silly as a child. When she opened her eyes a few moments later, she was alone. Siko had disappeared.

Aling Saturnina got up slowly. Her legs were stiff. Her back ached. The thought struck her that she was already very old, that she would not have long to live. She hurried back to the village. How long had the dogs been silent? It was dark and peaceful in the little hut she shared with Ana, Poldo, and their two children. In the corner of the one room, a votive candle cast its reddish light on the painting of Christ which Ana had propped up on a table. Garlands of dried flowers hung from the painting's upper corners. Carefully, so as not to wake the sleepers, *Aling* Saturnina groped her way forward. Kneeling before the makeshift altar, *Aling* Saturnina gazed long and hard at the face, so foreign in its whiteness, staring back at her. The nose was long and sharp, the lips thin and straight. The long, brown hair fell in fantastic curls past the white-robed shoulders. *Aling* Saturnina clasped her hands. She wanted to pray for Siko and Lina, and for the rest of her children, who she imagined must be suffering, just as Siko and Lina had suffered.

"*Aman namin*," she prayed. "*Aman namin...*"

But that was as far as she went, for she had forgotten the rest of the words to the Lord's Prayer. She gazed, helpless and mute, at the painting before her. Ah, she was unworthy, she had not been taught the proper words with which to couch her requests. For a little donation, perhaps the priest in San Pablo could be induced to say a mass for her children. How had she dared to raise her voice to God—she, who had proven to be such an unfit mother! For such impertinence she should be struck by lightning! Filled with remorse, she cowered for a few moments before the amiable gaze of the Christ in the painting.

Slowly, before she realized it, her eyelids began to droop. Then she gave a tired sigh and her shoulders sagged. *Aling* Saturnina was fast asleep.

Early the next morning, a cloud of dust could be seen rolling at high speed down the narrow road that led to the village. The cloud would stop suddenly before a particularly deep pothole, the dust would subside, and the outline of an army jeep could be briefly seen before being swallowed up again in a fresh cloud of dust. Just before the village, the jeep stopped, and four men in tight-fitting military uniforms stepped out. The villagers remained in their homes, peering watchfully from the windows. The four men paused at the first house they came to, the home of *Mang* Tomas. After briefly stopping to ask for directions, they continued down the street until they arrived at the house of *Aling* Saturnina. One of the men approached the ladder leading up to the house. The other three remained standing near the road. Before the man near the ladder could ascend, *Aling* Saturnina's face, stiff with suspicion, appeared at a window.

"What do you want?" she said.

"Are you the mother of Francisco Dawang?" the man by the ladder inquired.

"I have no son by that name," *Aling* Saturnina said angrily, and made to shut the window.

"Wait, *Ale*! Don't be so impatient. We know that Francisco Dawang, also known as Siko, was indeed your son. We just need you to answer a few questions."

"I have not seen Siko in over ten years," *Aling* Saturnina said. "And I curse the day I bore him."

"He was shot breaking into someone's house last night in San Pablo. We have another one of your children, Lina, in the jail. Won't you please come along quietly now?"

At the mention of Lina's name, *Aling* Saturnina seemed to waver. She disappeared from the window a moment and the men could hear her speaking to someone inside the house. Finally she reappeared at the door, tying a worn bandanna around her head.

"All right," she said. "I'll come. But I have to be back by nightfall, you hear?"

"Of course, *Ale*," one of the men said. "It's only a formality."

They tried to help her down the stairs, but she waved them away angrily. Then she walked quickly away from the house, not bothering to glance at any of the neighbors, who were peering from their windows.

When they had almost reached the jeep, they heard a voice calling, "Wait! Wait!" They all turned and looked. It was Ana, running down the road with her youngest child balanced on her hip.

"I'm coming, too!" Ana cried. "I can't let my mother go alone."

"*Stupida!*" *Aling* Saturnina shouted. "Go home and wait for Poldo to get back from the fields."

Ana paused only long enough to hand her child to the astonished wife of *Mang* Tomas, who was watching from her front gate.

"*Ale*, tell Poldo I've accompanied *Ina* to town. Tell him not to worry about me, I'll be back this evening."

Aling Saturnina continued to protest. "Idiot!" she berated her daughter. "You'd leave your own children!"

"Quiet!" one of the soldiers said. "We'll bring her along, too."

Aling Saturnina grew dazed and silent. She and Ana got into the jeep, the engine roared to life, the soldiers leaped in, and soon they were far away; there was nothing to see along the narrow road but the dust steaming up from the potholes. It was quiet in the village again. *Mang* Tomas's wife cradled Ana's baby in her arms. "Shush, shush," she whispered, for it was crying.

The next morning, when *Aling* Saturnina and Ana had not returned, Poldo went into town to make inquiries. That night he returned alone, looking like a much older man than the one who had set out in the morning. He had been directed to various military offices, and at each one was told that the two had been turned over to the National Bureau of Investigation "for further questioning." The time for harvesting rice came and went, and still *Aling* Saturnina and her daughter did not return.

Poldo and his two children live alone now in the house behind the *santol* tree. The children, seven and four, are very thin and are always crying for their mother. Poldo continues to go into town to make inquiries, but his trips are becoming more infrequent.

Poldo himself is gaunt and quiet, not at all like his former self. The villagers can remember a time when he could plant more rice saplings in a day than any other man in the village. Now they look sadly at him as he toils alone in the fields and note how, when he presses against the heavy wooden plow, his ribs create ridges on his chest and back. He is too thin, almost tubercular. Who will take care of his children if he goes?

In the meantime, Siko's ghost continues to roam the village. Several times the villagers have begged the parish priest from San Pablo to come and exorcise him, but each time the parish priest replies that he is too busy. The ghost can sometimes be seen dancing across the rice paddies on nights when there is a full moon, or sitting on the roof of someone's house, glaring with reddish eyes. In the beginning, the villagers tried to chase him away with holy water and crucifixes. He would disappear for a few days and then return. Now they merely shrug their shoulders. He has been absorbed into the pattern of their everyday existence. He is as familiar to them now as the air they breathe or the water they drink. They tell their children that he is a *tikbalang*, a creature who makes his home in the forest and who likes to play tricks on people. They avert their eyes from the shadows when walking alone at night. They have learned to live with the ghost, as they have learned to live with everything else, as they have learned to smile, to shrug, when pigs or chickens disappear, saying only, "It is Siko."

Grandmother

They say my mother is crazy. They say she married my father when he was just eighteen and she was already an older woman of thirty-two. They say my father was no good, that he stole. He was in jail once, for stealing from a rich widow in San Pablo. My grandmother says, what did my mother have to get married for? She had a good job as a cook with a rich family in Manila. But she came home one year for vacation, met my father, and then had me.

My grandmother says my father was a devil. Where he came from, no one knows. He walked into town, barefoot, in the middle of the dry season. One of his eyes was all black, as though there were a hole there instead of an eye. He passed my mother as she was drawing water from the pump. She stared at him. From then on, my grandmother says, my mother couldn't have enough of him.

My grandmother says she tried to warn my mother, but my mother was stubborn. My grandmother and my mother fought about my father all the time, until finally my mother took my father with her to Manila, to work for the rich family. But they caught him stealing one day and threw him out. My mother followed because she was pregnant with my younger brother.

My grandmother is very old. Her face is dark and wrinkled, and if she were not my grandmother I would even say that she is ugly. The veins on the backs of her hands are like tree roots. Her eyes have a milky-white film over the black parts. She moves slowly, because of her lame foot, but she is still strong. Every day she sweeps the yard with her broom of wooden bristles, and takes our clothes down to the river where she washes them, slapping them against the smooth stones. We are afraid of her hard hands, the palms like shoe leather, which bruise our arms, our cheeks. Even when we are far away we hear her voice, sharp and angry, arguing with the neighbors. When she calls us for our supper, we know we have to come running, or she will twist our ears and perhaps give us a slap or two.

Before we came, she lived by herself in her one-room *nipa* hut way off at the edge of San Ysidro. She doesn't go into town much—only on market days—and even then she has a scowl on her face. I sometimes wonder why she is always so angry, but then I tell myself she can't help it; it is because she is thinking of my mother. Every day I hear her muttering my mother's name to herself. At times she spits it out like a curse.

My younger brother Ipe, who my grandmother says looks so much like my father, is always hungry. She doesn't give him as much food as she gives me. Ipe says he will run away as soon as he gets a little bigger. He says he saw our father once, standing behind the mango tree at the back of our hut. This man had one black eye and feet that were wide and flat, like lily pads. He called to Ipe and Ipe would have gone, only just then a big black dog came along and Ipe, remembering what my grandmother says about such animals, got scared and ran instead to the hut where my grandmother was cooking rice. When he told grand-mother about the man, she grew even angrier than she always is and grabbed her big wooden spoon—the one that she uses to ladle out soup—and said she would hit my father over the head with it if he came any nearer. Then she wouldn't let Ipe go out any-more, but kept him by her side all day, with her rosary around his neck as though to ward off some evil.

I know my father is dead, but I don't tell Ipe. They say it happened a long time ago, before Ipe could even walk. It was the time of the last drought, when there was no food and my mother had just left us to look for work in Manila. They say my father got into a fight with a man from the next town and that man stuck my father in the back with a big *bolo*. Then, since no one liked my father, they left him in the middle of the street until he died. They say he took a long time, and just before he went, he got to his feet, arched his back, and gave a howl that reached all the way to Cavite. Afterward, his back remained arched and no one could straighten him out enough to fit into a coffin. So they simply dug a hole in the ground and left him there.

People have started to say things about my mother—about why she has not come back to San Ysidro for so long. They say she has taken up with another man, that she has left Manila and now works in a bar in Olongapo, where the American servicemen are. They say she is touched in the head, man-crazy. It all began when she was fifteen and her first *nobyo*, the one she probably would have been happy with, the townspeople say, was struck by lightning as he was coming home from working in the fields. He was burnt black, as black as the statue of the Nazarene in the main altar of the parish church. Afterward, when my mother took up with my father, who had that one black eye, they said the ghost of her first lover was still haunting her, that she could never get over him.

I hear all these things from my grandmother. I wonder how she knows what she does, but I am afraid to ask. My grandmother, too, has no husband. Or maybe she had one once, but it was too long ago to make any difference. There are many women like her in the town, women whose husbands have left them to work in the big city, and whose children seem to spring—bones, skin, hair, and all—entirely from their mother's loins.

Yet my grandmother was a good mother. She was the one who watched over my mother when she nearly lost her mind over her young man, when he was struck by lightning. People said my mother couldn't be left alone, that she had to be watched day and night, because she had almost succeeded in drowning herself in the river. Then my grandmother brought my mother to an *herbolario* who made my mother lie down on a table and pulled bushels and bushels of dried brown leaves out of my mother's mouth, and after that my mother began to feel much better. She stopped talking about her dead *nobyo* and found a good job in the city and my grandmother had no more trouble from her for many years.

That is why this thing with my father was so bad. My grandmother did not like my father at all, not at all. But what could she do? The more my grandmother talked about my father, the less my mother listened, until finally it was as if my grandmother were nothing but a rock or a tree, that was how little attention my mother paid her. My grandmother says that when my mother wanted a man, she was like someone under a spell. Her breath always came a little faster, she grew pale, she even gave off a smell. If you have seen the stray dogs wandering around our village, how they behave when they are in heat, going around all day rubbing against posts and scratching themselves, that was how my mother would be.

That was how she was when I was little, a very long time ago, before I even heard that my father had died. We were already living with my grandmother then, and my mother was going around San Ysidro in tight jeans and high heels, powdering her face even for trips to the pump. At mass no one sat beside us in the pews, nor did my mother ask for the priest's blessing as we filed in front of him before leaving the church.

Nights were hard. My mother and grandmother would fight. They always stood outside the hut when they thought we were sleeping. But I would creep to the window and look out, and I would see them in the yard under the mango tree. It was mostly my grandmother who did the talking at such times. I tried to hear what she was saying, but even when I could hear, the words had no meaning. What did I know of such words, words like "morals" and "virtue" and "piety," words that could hurt my mother? Evil words—words that made my mother stoop, as though there were a great weight pressing on her back. Afterward, my mother would lie down on the mat beside me, and I would carefully pat the curve of her back, feeling the thin bones beneath her duster, and know that she was crying.

Now she has gone away again, back to the big city. Now when I go into town, people look at me and shake their heads. I see their lips form words: "Poor girl." It is as though they think my mother is not coming back. They say my grandmother is angry because my mother has stopped sending money. I used to see thin, pale blue envelopes, so light they seemed to be filled with air, behind the portrait of the Sacred Heart of Jesus on the shelf. Now nothing is there, and my grandmother beats Ipe almost everyday. Ipe cries, makes his hand a fist, and presses it against his mouth. Afterward, he will sit in the mango tree and look out over the fields. I hear him saying, as if to our father, "Come and get me. I am ready now."

Memorial

The city of Manila abounded with graffiti artists. Conditions were good—there was a dictatorship, a fifty percent rate of inflation, and drought in the provinces.

Some graffiti artists liked to work in small spaces, such as in public urinals, library carrels, and even on the pages of library books. Their graffiti consisted mostly of poetic statements.

There were others whose work consisted solely of political slogans. These were the truly daring ones. They wrote, "Down with the dictatorship of_____!" or "Down with the Ministry of _____!" knowing full well that if one were caught writing such things on a wall one was immediately taken to Camp Crame or Camp Aguinaldo and was never heard from again.

Lately, there had been a series of headlines in the government-run newspaper that dealt with the executions of leading members of the New People's Army. Only the names varied. One week it would be: JOCSON KILLED. The next week it would be: ONGPIN KILLED. And so forth. Not a week went by without the appearance of at least one _____ KILLED headline.

Certain kinds of graffiti artists were kept busy by this sort of thing. They were known as "memorialists." Whenever anyone disappeared or was reported missing, or whenever a leader of the New People's Army had been killed, one would be sure to find a commemorative sketch somewhere, drawn with brightly colored chalk, calling the government to account.

Fernando Fajardo was a memorialist. Before becoming a memorialist, he was a painter, famous in particular for a series of nudes he modeled after his late wife. These were of such quality that the critics began referring to him as "the next Amorsolo." Well, what happened? First, he turned sixty. Then, like lava, like a force of nature, came the realization that society had not gotten any better; that in fact, in many respects, it was getting worse.

The government was always announcing the start of a new campaign—the "Good Grooming Campaign" of a few years back when all young men who wore their hair below their shirt collars were herded into Camp Crame and threatened with confinement, and the "Campaign for Truth and Beauty," which coincided with the opening of the first University of Life, where regular courses were replaced by courses on the president's philosophy. And there had even been an "Anti-Vice Campaign," when secret marshals went around shooting anyone with a tattoo, on the assumption that they were all hardened criminals. But in the streets there were still little children who pressed their gaunt faces right up against the windows of cars when they stopped at intersections, so that the snot from their flattened noses rubbed off on the glass, and one could see the threads of milky-white moisture at the corners of their runny eyes. Boys with green eye make-up and little girls with reddened lips lurked behind the old Baclaran church at night, whispering: "Hey mister, you like me? You want me?"

One warm night, not long after his birthday, Fajardo was walking home from a dinner party at a friend's house. It was close to the Lenten season—all the doors he passed were decorated with palm-leaf crosses that people had brought with them to mass that morning for blessing by the priests. The moon shone white and full; a breeze blew in from the river, bringing with it the smell of roasted peanuts from some unseen vendor's cart. He could hear distant voices, shouting and laughter, but they were too far away for him to make out what they were saying. A familiar feeling came over him—a feeling, almost, of grief.

He reminded himself to be careful and keep his eyes down as he walked. The streets were full of potholes, some deep enough for a child to play in, and the pavement had buckled up in many places. There were no functioning street lights either, in this part of the city. Perhaps that was why, even on this warm and fragrant evening, he was the only person out; everyone else was shut up tight in their homes.

At one time, Fajardo remembered, the city had been very beautiful. There had been old houses by the river, houses left over from Spanish times, with tiled roofs and balconies overlooking the water. People liked to sit out on their balconies in the late afternoon, sipping cool drinks made from mango or guayabano. There had been trees along the sidewalks, and gas street lamps that gave the whole area the feeling of a park. But now the water of the river was brown and muddy; people said this was because the government had constructed a glass factory just upstream.

He stopped and gazed at the riverfront. Off to one side, he remembered, there used to be a children's park, with slides and swings, and just a little further on, around the next corner, there had been a park with benches, where he used to meet his wife when she was still a *colegiala*. A *taho* vendor passing by just then with two heavy tin cans balanced on a bamboo pole across his shoulders, stopped and stared.

"What do you find to look at in the river, *Tatang*?" the man asked. He was a very old man, with sad eyes and a sunken, tubercular chest.

"I am remembering a time when the water here was clear, when it was possible to fish," Fajardo explained.

The man simply stared, and if anyone had asked him he would have stated emphatically that he did not believe there had ever been such a time.

Fajardo walked on. He was getting closer to his home. He thought of the cup of hot chocolate he would prepare in the kitchen, and the warm bed that awaited him afterward. He began to walk quickly. Without realizing it, he had become tired. The party, the long walk, the thoughts that filled his head, all conspired to make him feel heavy, as though there were something pressing on his shoulders. He could feel the little case of chalk in the right breast pocket of his worn coat. It knocked against his chest, as if in entreaty. But he was tired. He had to stop at certain points and wipe the perspiration from the back of his neck.

Was it only the previous night he had begun writing the sentence? It had come to him, with startling clarity, when he was sitting in his evening bath. The words spoke volumes: *YOU ARE NOT ALONE.* He had been writing it everywhere since then: on pillars underneath the overpass, on blank concrete walls, on hollow block structures beneath government postings that said: *Bawal Umihi Dito.*

But who was he speaking to? Was he speaking to the people he saw in the market, or to the cawing birds flying over the bay, or to the silently crying beggar children who knocked against the car windows? He did not know.

When he first wrote the words, he felt the wall beneath his fingers seem to come alive, almost to breathe. He had to press his palms flat, let the cold stone assert its reality, to rid himself of the notion that the city was talking to HIM, that he was in turn talking to the city. Now he knew there was a message there somewhere, a message of hope and renewal. But he was not one to analyze. He wrote because he had to.

He continued on his way home. Here and there he encountered a stray corpse. Since most wore tattoos, he assumed they were victims of the Anti-Vice Campaign. There was also the odd unmarked corpse—a journalist, perhaps, or a lawyer—buried surreptitiously among the weeds. It was easy to tell what they were because of their slight builds and pale complexions, as though all their lives had been spent shut up in close, dark rooms. He assumed they had been guilty of a political indiscretion.

Once, however, he found the body of a young girl. She could not have been more than thirteen or fourteen years old. She was half-clothed, and there was a trickle of something that looked like blood but that he later ascertained was mercurochrome, running from her mouth down her throat. From the plaid pattern on her torn skirt he guessed she had been a student at the Assumption Convent.

These were the girls who flitted in groups all over the shopping malls, with braided hair and socks and shiny patent leather shoes. They were a bright spot in the otherwise dull and shabby urban landscape. He could hear their high voices around him in the *turo-turos* where he liked to eat. He liked to watch them gossiping in corners, their hands moving expressively through the air.

No matter how jaded the city populace had become, these young girls seemed untouched. Most of them lived privileged lives, being driven around by chauffeurs, learning French from European nuns, getting their houseboys to buy Blue Seal cigarettes for them on the sly.

But this one girl had gone astray. She had gotten mixed up in something terrible. Perhaps she had a brother or a boyfriend who had become "political." The authorities were ruthless even to those not directly involved.

This corpse moved Fajardo more than the others, and he gave her a name: "Maganda," which in old Tagalog legends was the name given to the first woman and meant "beautiful." Actually, when Fajardo found her, she had her teeth knocked out and her nose broken, so it was difficult for anyone to say then that she was beautiful, but despite what had been done to her, he guessed that she must have been beautiful.

The walls that once enclosed the young girl's body were almost completely covered with his sketches. On the far wall, the one parallel to the street, he made a rough drawing of an execution: the falling figure of a man done in black chalk, three parallel lines across his torso representing ropes, three white columns, representing soldiers, in the distance. Next to that he sketched a gigantic face with heavily marked eyebrows, a blur of dark chalk for a mouth, and a crown of laurel leaves. He meant this to be Agatep, the university student who was killed only the previous week, during the government's latest push into the Sierra Madre. He considered writing a dedication, but eventually decided against it because it would mean certain reprisal. And he wanted to go on making sketches. One simply had to be clever, to use symbols, to state nothing outright. He was proud, in fact, that so far no one had thought fit to erase his drawings, that they had survived the scrutiny of the censors.

Fajardo hurried home. His mind was full. He thought of the party he had just left, and of the people he had seen there—old professors mostly, from the University of the Philippines. He did not really like going to these gatherings. There were inevitably arguments, and he always ended up drinking too much. But he could not do without the talk; it was for this reason only that he attended such gatherings. People could always be relied upon to say something that amazed him.

One of the people there was an old professor named Avansena. People made fun of him, said his mind was gone. He was a very stubborn old man and stated his opinions very loudly and forcefully, so everyone was forced to listen to him. This evening he had been full of talk of a certain Balweg. Some item he'd read in the paper—the government was pushing deep into the Kalinga-Apayao region, a wild place, where few people from Manila have ever been.

"You cannot imagine it," Avansena said. "I was there years ago, as a young man. The people who live in those valleys move about the mountains like goats. They are short, stocky people. Their feet are hoofed. They hardly ever speak."

People did not know whether to laugh. But it was an interesting story; no one tried to stop Avansena from telling it.

"There is a priest there," Avansena had continued. "His name is Balweg. He is a wild man—strong, strong as a *tamaraw*. He is one of the mountain people. He has joined the New People's Army. No bullets can touch him. The soldiers are fleeing from the hills; they don't want to fight a representative of God. They say it is God who directs his bullets. He himself has not even a scratch."

Fajardo had wanted Avansena to continue. But there was a government man there. A friend of Avansena's took him aside and reminded him of the other man's presence. The government man had turned an ugly shade of red. He was angry. But he could not do anything except mutter: "Stupid, senile old man!"

Now Fajardo had reached his gate. The latch made a horrible grating sound that echoed off the courtyard walls, and the old caretaker, *Mang* Felipe, woke grudgingly from his corner and came forward unsteadily, accompanied by his two barking mongrels. Inside, Fajardo exchanged a few words with *Mang* Felipe, then began to climb the stairs leading to his quarters. He could no longer see the moon or smell the river. Soon he was in his bed, fast asleep.

When Fajardo awoke, he saw sunlight streaming in through the window and heard the twitter of birds, sounding impossibly close. He was momentarily confused by the sight of his clothes scattered across the bedroom floor. Then he remembered the walk home through the dark streets, in the warm night, with the soft wind from the Pasig blowing against his back, and his brief conversation with the *taho* vendor.

He had not slept easily. He had dreamt of people he had not seen for a very long time. He remembered one image in particular, the image of his dead wife, and in this dream she seemed very close, seemed, almost, about to touch him as he lay on the bed. Awake, he thought he could still feel her comforting presence, like an arm around his neck. It seemed to him that he caught just the faintest trace of a sigh in the room, a whisper, as though his wife had spoken and just this minute walked out the door. She seemed to say, "Ay, Fernando," and the tone of her voice was one of sadness and exasperation. Often she had sounded like that, when she was alive.

They had not had any children. "If I had a son," Fajardo thought now, "I would make sure he would not forget us. I would tell him: Visit our graves on All Saints' Day, and bring food and candles, and hold vigils there with your wife and children. Do not forget us!"

Then he shivered, feeling something cold pressing down. Was that a feather, now brushing his right ear? He put out a hand, but grasped only air.

After a few moments, he rose heavily, walked to the front steps and retrieved the morning paper. It was a thick paper, with very small, almost illegible print. An item on one of the inside pages caught his eye:

> *The army has launched the largest military offensive against leftist guerrillas since rebel activity began in the mountains of the north, a provincial military commander said Saturday. Among the military's targets was a fugitive Roman Catholic priest, wanted dead or alive, with a price on his head.*
>
> *Soldiers pursuing rebels in the Kalinga area Friday captured a guerrilla camp and found documents and ammunition hastily abandoned by retreating rebels. Military sources say among the fleeing rebels was the Rev. Conrado Balweg, a priest from the nearby province of Abra, who joined the rebels in 1979. Balweg is the former parish priest of Luba, a mountain town about 180 miles northwest of Manila. He belongs to the Igorot tribe, whose 700,000 members live on the slopes and valleys of the Cordilleras. The military has offered a reward of 400,000 pesos ($22,222) for Balweg, dead or alive. The military has set up checkpoints on roads leading to the Cordilleras area and travellers are being searched.*

For a long time, Fajardo remained seated at the table. His bowed head scarcely moved. It hung over the page, as though suspended. He seemed to be reading. But he was, in actuality, dreaming.

That night was cool like the previous night, and the box of chalk in his inside coat pocket knocked comfortably against his chest like an old friend. The streets were empty and his footsteps echoed. Rounding a corner, he again saw the *taho* vendor, leaning morosely against a wall. He nodded his head in greeting, and the man simply stared at him with hollow eyes. Fajardo hurried on without speaking.

The vacant lot was undisturbed. In the moonlight, his sketches seemed to breathe, or perhaps it was simply his failing eyesight that lent them a quality of faint movement.

He walked around, examining more closely what he had done. That was when he saw the other words, written in an inconspicuous corner, words that went straight to his heart: *IT HURTS ME, TOO.*

The lettering was small and cramped. In places, where the rough limestone of the wall rose, the letters seemed to fade. The line slanted downward, as though the man or woman writing had gotten tired of supporting his or her arm. The last letter was incomplete, the "o" almost like a "u." He touched the letters reverently, and felt moisture. He thought, inexplicably, of tears. Yet the chalk was dry.

Some bits of orange chalk were still lying on the ground. He collected them carefully and put them in his pocket. He looked among the weeds, but saw nothing out of the ordinary. He thought of going home. He did not feel safe any longer, knowing someone else had discovered the place. But something made him stop. It was an image that had been on his mind all day. It called to him now, insistently.

After kneeling a long while on the damp ground, he came to a decision. He prepared his chalk. He began to sketch a mountain.

The next night, there was again something new. This time, it was—*THE WILL OF THE DICTATOR.*

Fajardo did not know what to make of it. He became truly frightened, so frightened his knees shook. The letters were large and covered nearly the entire lower half of one wall. Again he debated whether to leave immediately. But his sketch of the mountain called to him. For a long time he stood hesitating. He thought of morning and the sun, and the river glinting, and barges floating. He thought of hot *pandesal*, and steaming mugs of bitter coffee. He felt the cold and the hard ground underneath his feet. Finally, with trembling hands, he took out his box of chalk.

"I must at least finish what I have started," he told himself.

By this time you are wondering: where does it all end? How many sketches does a man have to make before the censors eventually take notice? It doesn't matter whether it is one or one hundred and one. What matters is that it all ends inevitably.

Fajardo's end was no more horrible than others. Ask anyone and they will tell you that he was taken away. Some *taho* vendor—

six children to feed at home, wife pregnant again with the seventh and raving—had reported him.

Fajardo was not aware of the forces that had been set in motion by the simple act of reading a four-inch newspaper item. He did not know how a man, bent over a kitchen table with a cup of hot chocolate in his right hand, can seem to swell and grow so that he no longer resembles himself but becomes something Other, something that as yet has no name. He only knew that a very complicated system of reactions were set off by the act of reading. It began with his eyes, which transmitted impulses that electrified his whole body, so that he trembled and could no longer hold his cup, so that he had to fold his arms in front of his chest and hold in whatever was inside him that threatened to spill out and engulf the entire room.

That last night, the night he was arrested, he had just begun a new sketch when the constabulary appeared. He had begun to sketch the figure of a man on a mountain, but he hadn't been able to finish much more than the jagged shapes of the mountain, and what looked to be the man's head.

It was clear who he was memorializing. It was that rebel priest, Balweg, the one who was killed just the other week in Benguet province. The police were very proud of that kill. They kept the body, they say. Just to show off.

ARMY KILLS REBEL CLERIC read the front page headline of the newspaper, the morning after Fajardo's arrest.

For a while, people wondered what happened to Fajardo. The neighbors remembered how he used to stand at the riverfront and mutter crazy things. He always went around with that box of chalk. But he was so old. Surely the old can be humored for their eccentricities. He was always kind, always ready to loan money to a neighbor or a friend. When his apartment remained empty, people started to say, "Was it possible—?" No one liked to think it.

The years went by. Avansena did not forget. He had cataracts in both eyes, he could barely walk, but he did not forget. One day, he went back to the place where Fajardo had made his last sketch. It was very quiet there, and the *talahib* grew quite tall. Who knew what snakes and scorpions were hiding in the tall grass? But the old man went bravely forward. He saw someone had written an epitaph on the wall, an epitaph that broke his heart. It said: WE WILL NEVER FORGET YOU, FERNANDO FAJARDO.

Ginseng

My father is 83. Once he was very handsome, but now he has plump hips and breasts, with dark, pointed nipples on top of two triangles of brown, leathery skin. It is impossible for me to think of him as still a man in the usual sense, in the sense he has wanted me to think of him for so many years.

It bothers me to watch him eat. He has a very good appetite, which is perhaps why he no longer bothers with knife and fork but greedily eats with his fingers. He can't bear to leave anything on his plate. When we have chicken thighs or spare ribs, he gnaws them down to the bone. Afterward, he will lick his fingers and say what a good meal that was—he wishes there was more.

My next door neighbor, Dr. Marcelo, says it's not good for him to eat as much as he does. Cholesterol, Dr. Marcelo says. But what can we do? Once, my wife Mara teased him about eating so much. My father was deeply offended and did not speak to her for a week. He tried to eat less at dinner, but later we would see him sneak into the kitchen when he thought no one was looking and begin to poke among the jars in the refrigerator with his walking stick.

Then he got sick. First he had stomach cramps and lay curled up in bed all day moaning. Then he started throwing up black clots and we had to call Dr. Marcelo. When Dr. Marcelo asked what he had eaten last, we really couldn't say; he'd been spending a lot of time in the kitchen, opening jars and putting bits of food he had fished out with his fingers into his mouth.

Dr. Marcelo said he thought it might be a case of food poisoning. He said it with an edge to his voice, as though we were somehow responsible. But is it our fault if this man can't distinguish between what is good for him and what isn't?

Neither of us can remember exactly when the changes began—when he started losing, little by little, the essential components of his personality. I think it began right after *Mamang's* death but Mara says no, it began later, when he began to miss the things *Mamang* used to do for him. She remembers the time we heard him sobbing in the bathroom and found him sitting naked in the tub. The soap had slipped and he couldn't reach for it. He was embarrassed because we saw him naked. That was when we discovered he had breasts.

Now he is only a collection of obsessions. He exists in a straight line, as though the only things that matter are the things that concern himself. We think his appetite is connected to the fact that he wants to go on living. It would not surprise us if he were to say one day, "I want to taste the heart of the banana palm." The old women say that the heart of the banana palm restores youth. In our backyard, near the creek that divides our property from *Mang* Felipe's, is a grove of these palms. We feel sure that one day he will ask us to chop one of them down, and then it will be no use our telling him that the old women are only telling stories, that the thread of his life is irrevocably wound up, that there is nothing any of us can do about it.

Much of my father's present condition has to do with things that happened a long time ago, before I was born—that peculiar time in Philippine history when the colony was changing hands. Mother Spain was out and the New World, America, was in. The old truths—the truths people had accepted for three hundred years—were exposed for the bits of trash they really were. Way back then, no one knew that they stood on the threshold of anything. The world of Manila was still the Spanish world of the *zarzuela* and the horse-drawn carriage. In that world, all it took to be a big man was a family line you could trace directly back to the old country, and features that testified to a Spanish patrimony.

The year 1900 was an important year. That was the year my father returned from Barcelona with a medical degree. My grandfather set him up in an office in one of the small side streets near the Chinese quarter of Manila. After hanging a brass plate with his name and the appellation "Doctor" outside his door, my father spent most of his time promenading in the park and drinking hot chocolate at his favorite cafe.

Mamang was the daughter of a Chinese shopkeeper. Every day my father passed her shop on his way to the office. *Mamang* noticed his bright, black eyes, his wavy hair pungent with brilliantine. He would walk down the street swinging a stick. The stick made hard, rhythmic taps on the pavement. After a while it seemed to *Mamang* that she could hear this tapping from a long way off, even before my father turned the corner into her street.

Mamang had small, shrewd eyes and a face that was broad like the moon, enclosed between two clouds of black hair. She was the second daughter. Her older sister had many suitors, but *Mamang* had none. She used to sit all day behind a counter, tallying up accounts on an abacus. She had long, lovely fingers. They moved gently over the worn beads making soft, clicking sounds. Sometimes, she would stop, put her hand to her cheek, and smile. People who saw her said she was wishing for a lover.

Mamang's father sold tea—oolong, ginseng, and jasmine. The tea came in red hexagonal canisters decorated with pictures of green mountains. Sometimes, when *Mamang*'s father brought out a special tea for a customer to examine, the smell was so strong that it wafted all the way out into the street. If my father happened to be passing by just then, he would glance curiously at the shop window, with its display of hanging scrolls and bamboo fans and bright, red canisters. After a while, the smell of tea came to seem very pleasant to him, and he looked forward to passing that shop every day on his way to the office.

My father came into the shop one day and asked *Mamang* to show him some tea. He didn't like the ones she showed him first, the tea her father imported from Longjing, China, that filled the room with a bitter odor. Then she showed him a tea made from aged ginseng root that smelled faintly of burnt sugar. When my father put it to his nose, it reminded him, unaccountably, of Barcelona. It was then, after smelling the tea, that *Mamang* began to look different to him. He began to notice her glistening, blue-black hair and her tiny feet and hands. He saw that while she wrapped up his order in rough, brown paper, her hands seemed to be caressing something very fine. He saw that though she said nothing, she would sometimes stop, touch her cheek, and smile. My father found all this enchanting.

People said that *Mamang* put a spell on my father. They said her fingers, moving delicately over the abacus beads, were those of a conjurer. They said her father had taught her which herbs were good for pain, sorrow, desire. My father, in later years, liked to tell people that he was bewitched. He said that he thought *Mamang* was a beautiful girl, but she turned out to be an ugly old crone.

As soon as he reached home, my father put the box of tea on his nightstand. He went to bed and slept badly. The room seemed very warm. When he awoke the next morning, he found himself wrapped up completely in the blanket and sheets, mummy-fashion. He saw the box of tea on the stand and thought again of *Mamang*. From then on, he could not keep from stopping by the teashop every day on his way to the office.

After a while, *Mamang*'s stomach began to swell. When it became clear that she was pregnant, everyone said "Ah!" and shook their heads knowingly. *Mamang*'s father moaned and cursed. He beat her with his bamboo cane but her belly continued to grow. Finally even her face became bloated. Her toes were so swollen she could no longer put on her black cloth slippers. She waited for my father to say something but he merely walked around wearing a mournful air.

My father had a secret, a monstrous secret, that was hard and round like a lump of black clay and weighed on his conscience. The truth was that he could never marry *Mamang* because my grandfather, who gave him a generous allowance that permitted him to spend all his afternoons promenading in the park and drinking hot chocolate at his favorite cafe, threatened to cut him off. Therefore he had to make a very indelicate proposition to *Mamang*, one that he would never have dared make to a woman of his own class.

One day, my father appeared at the teashop to take *Mamang* away. *Mamang*'s father stood on the sidewalk and shook his fist at him, but my father only looked impassively at the shopkeeper's large yellow teeth flecked with saliva, and at his bony, tubercular chest. He stood out on the street, waiting for *Mamang* to get her things together. When she finally came, moving very slowly because she was so big but also because she was crying, my father put her in a carriage and they went to a nice little apartment he had found for her in a secluded section of the city. There *Mamang* spent most of her time ironing my father's fine linen shirts and starching his collars. In the mornings she ran the hot water for his bath and put out the clothes and shoes he was to wear that day.

When he was fully dressed, with a safari hat on his head and a walking stick in his right hand, he looked very distinguished. People who saw him promenading in the park often mistook him for a magistrate.

Mamang stayed home. After a long time, her hair turned white. She became old and ugly. My father had many other women, but *Mamang* always waited for him to come back to her. The last time he came back was after an absence of several years. He was old himself. He had a cataract in one eye. He and *Mamang* cried together—cried because so much had happened and they were not, either of them, the better for it.

Mamang told me these things before she died. I sat by her bed in the close, dark room in the early evenings, watching the sun disappear behind the roofs of the neighboring houses. While the room grew darker and darker, *Mamang*'s voice would gather strength. She would turn her head from side to side and curse at people long gone. But she never spoke out against my father. "What could he do?" she would say. "He was the son of a rich man. They used to call his father *'El Señor.'* He never had to work and he didn't know how to. What could he do?"

Toward the end, she grew much thinner and shorter and even a little hunchbacked. Any kind of food seemed to make her nauseous. One day we discovered her sitting in her usual chair by the window, her hands folded together on her lap. Her eyes were closed; she looked as though she were only sleeping. We were frightened because we had never actually seen her with her eyes closed and now she looked different. We began to notice that her nose was hooked and pointed and that her skin was bad. Then, because we didn't want to look any more, we began to sing and clap our hands, like children trying to ward off the Beast. Or perhaps we already knew and were trying to call her soul back, trying to make her change her mind about leaving us.

We were so frightened that night we climbed into the big four-poster bed in her room and clung to each other. We waited until the next morning to call Dr. Marcelo, and when he came he looked at us in that way—that accusatory way he looked when he told us our father had food poisoning. His look, his thin dry voice, his long white fingers probing *Mamang* here and there terrified us.

"How long has she been sitting there?" he said, because of course we had not moved her.

We said, since yesterday. He didn't say anything more. By then we understood what was expected of us and Mara went to the phone to call the embalmers.

At *Mamang*'s funeral my father was quiet and subdued. He stood leaning heavily on his cane while people came up to him and pressed the back of his left hand to their foreheads in the traditional sign of respect. He murmured no words of greeting. He looked at everyone as though they were strangers. Afterward, it shocked us to realize that he hadn't known whose body it was in the fine mahogany coffin, that he had been standing there with the air of being present but was in fact unconscious of everything but the cold rain trickling down the insides of his new shoes. How else to interpret the look of vague irritation with which he observed the coffin being lowered into the ground, the sigh of relief he uttered when someone told him it was time to go?

We think that much of our present difficulty is *Mamang*'s fault. She shouldn't have died and left us to carry on alone—with him. We wonder sometimes why he is so very much alive, so very much there, and why it has to be *Mamang* in the ground, *Mamang*, whom we could count on to solve every difficulty. Sometimes, after dinner, when we are having a drink together in the den, we think we feel her presence and we look instinctively at her chair in the corner. But, of course, it is empty. Still, it is such feelings that restrain us from throwing him bodily out of the house.

The other day he said, "I am going to Barcelona." He was fully dressed and he even had his filthy old safari hat and his walking stick. He began walking out the door. "Ha, ha!" I said. "Mind you don't get run over crossing the street." He remained standing a long time by the door, as though he were trying to remember something. Finally, just when we were going to bed, Mara came and took him gently by the hand. "You're in Barcelona now," she told him.

One day we will discover that he is no longer a presence to us. Perhaps it will happen when we are sitting around the breakfast table and one of us will notice that no one has opened the jars in the refrigerator for a very long time. Or perhaps we will realize that we no longer listen carefully for the sound of sobbing from the bathroom. Then there will be a new sound in the house—sharp, penetrating. The sound a newborn baby makes when it has just come from its mother's belly. Mara says she wants it to happen. We both pray for a girl, if only so that we can say to one another that *Mamang* has been reborn.

The Insult

It was a hot August night in Manila, one of those nights when people spill out onto the streets because it is too hot indoors. Luneta Park teemed with people moving sluggishly across the withered, brown grass. Crowds jostled and pushed on the seawall along Roxas Boulevard, while children clambered among the rocks leading down to the water. Now and then a group would leave the seawall and head toward the hotels and nightclubs lining the boulevard from end to end.

Jackie Ortiz-Luiz shot a man that night—a murder of very little consequence. The victim was a movie actor named Bobby Bautista. In the heat of an argument Bautista had slapped Paloma, Jackie's sister, at a disco. So Jackie had shot him. Few felt sorry about it.

"He had it coming," some people said afterward. "He had some nerve to think he could get away with it."

The day after the event there was a little item in the paper, one column-inch long, tucked away at the bottom of page fifteen. If not looking carefully, one would have missed the item altogether. It said:

> *Bobby Bautista, the twenty-five-year-old movie actor who starred in the critically acclaimed films,* Hand of Fate *and* Child of the Morning, *was found dead in his house at 782 Mariano Marcos Street this morning. The cause of death appeared to be a self-inflicted gunshot wound. Beside the body was a handwritten note*

addressed to Bautista's parents. Friends said the actor had been suffering from recurring bouts of depression.

Nothing more was heard about Bobby Bautista. His family, far away in Davao Province, flew his body home and held their tongues. The directors at Sampaguita Pictures began a widely publicized talent search for a new face to star in the film Bautista had been working on when he died. After a few months, the mention of his name elicited only shrugs, and Bobby Bautista faded from memory.

In retrospect, Bautista was a poor, ignorant farm boy who made it big very fast in the movie business because a director happened to like his looks. He arrived in Manila from Davao with exactly forty-three *pesos* in the pocket of his faded blue denims and a battered old guitar he had inherited from his father. He began waiting on tables at a bar-restaurant on Mabini called The Fishnet. It was the kind of place where they occasionally asked the staff to get up and sing, and it happened that Bobby Bautista, with a voice that was pleasant enough to listen to, became quite popular there. The people who came to The Fishnet were mostly older men, and they liked the place because of the girls who served the drinks, and who occasionally agreed to be taken home for the night. It soon became clear that Bobby was attracting a different sort— quiet men who stayed in the corners of the room, smoking quietly and looking at him intently. Among these men was a director, a man named Rez Cortez.

Cortez was a short man with thinning hair that had once been black but was now dyed a light brown, a color that turned a rusty orange at the fringes. The fringes hung over his forehead, partially obscuring his eyes, which were watchful and reserved. He was only in his mid-thirties, but he had already directed close to thirty movies. At the time he met Bautista, he had a hit movie, and had been praised for resurrecting the career of an older actress, someone who'd been famous in the fifties. There was talk of a FAMAS award, and his picture appeared often in the tabloids.

The first time he came to The Fishnet, Bautista noticed him immediately. The waiters were deferential, taking the man's order before others who had been waiting longer.

Bautista began to wonder about the man. He wondered if the man could be of any use to him. Before he could finish his set, however, Cortez stood up. Tossing a few crumpled *pesos* on the table, he walked out. Bautista was keenly disappointed. For a moment he'd been tempted to follow the stranger out the door. But Bautista knew the man would be gone long before he could reach the entrance.

Afterward, Bautista questioned a few of the waiters. They looked at him strangely, but one of them finally said, "He's a director. I've seen his picture in *The Sun*. He asked a lot of questions about you." The other waiters joked privately about the man's sexual orientation.

In the days afterward, Bautista felt increasingly detached from his surroundings. If he did not look down very carefully at the pavement, and watch where he placed his feet, he would find himself knocking against lamp posts and railings, not realizing until later at night that he had actually bruised his elbows, his thighs. Things happened to him, but they made no impression.

Bautista could see clearly now how he could gain recognition and make a name for himself. He had to be incredibly lucky, but he believed that something would happen, that this man Cortez was going to help him.

He continued to sing every night, but he was not really aware of what he was doing or how he sounded. His eyes roved restlessly to the entrance. Then, one night, almost as if Bautista's will had summoned him, Cortez again walked into the bar.

Cortez came two nights a week for almost two months, always staying for Bautista's set. He sat by the door and talked to no one. He smoked thin brown cigarettes and stared at Bautista from the darkness. One night, as Bautista was leaving the stage, he saw Cortez beckon. When he approached, the director said, in a dry and faintly ironic voice, "How would you like to be in the movies?"

That was how Bautista started to gain recognition and make a name for himself. When his first movie was released a few months later, Bautista was a star.

Perhaps it was too much to expect that all these events unfolding so rapidly and seemingly so naturally had occurred purely by chance. That was why, when Bautista tried to analyze things, he thought he could see a pattern, a connecting thread. That he was special, different, far removed from the ordinary class of laborer who worked hard all his life and then died poor and miserable had been, he thought, apparent from the start. He had always been drawn to Manila, had always felt driven by a great hunger for what the city had to offer. His instincts told him that something awaited him here—something big and grand and beautiful.

He remembered how his mother wept when he told her he was leaving, how she prayed and lit candles before the statue of the Virgin in the Church of Saint Jude, the patron saint of lost causes. But none of it had done any good. Fate directed him to go to the city and he went. Fate decreed that Rez Cortez walk into the Fishnet when there were maybe fifty bars just like it all up and down A. Mabini Avenue, and fate had decreed that he, Bobby Bautista, a poor, struggling singer making barely enough to afford two meals a day, would wake up a few months later, a star. This to him was the undeniable truth.

People said he was *suwerte*—lucky—but he had one final answer for them. He had an amulet, a magic charm. The old folks called it *anting-anting* and said it endowed its wearer with special powers. It was only a round, smooth white stone the size of a marble. He had it in his pocket the night Cortez walked into the Fishnet, and every night after that he carried it with him. The night he saw Cortez beckon, he reached down and gave it a hasty rub with his right forefinger. And hadn't things turned out splendidly, better even than he dared to hope? The amulet was powerful, and the power was his. His mother had kept it for him, tucked away in a secret place. As a girl of seventeen she waited beneath a banana palm one moonlit night and saw the tree's leaves start to quiver and shake. Presently she saw a stone shoot forth from atop the crown of leaves and, mindful of what the old folks said, she opened her mouth and caught it on her tongue. Weeping, she pressed it into her son's hand the day he left Davao. Now it dangled from a gold chain around his neck.

Bautista had never owned a car in his life, but now the studio loaned him a $25,000 sportscar, imported from England, with a rear engine and doors that lifted up instead of out. He liked to strut around in a leather jacket and boots, even in the hottest weather. He ate at the most expensive restaurants, and entertained lavishly in his home. He tried to drop his Davao accent.

Bautista developed a taste for discos. His favorite was the Stargazer, on the top floor of the Holiday Inn on Roxas Boulevard. Here he spent his time drinking and exchanging lewd jokes with his cronies. Without realizing it, Bautista made himself an easy mark.

Paloma Ortiz-Luiz met Bautista there. Only nineteen, she'd been married once before. She had applied for a church annulment after only a year of marriage. It was whispered that she had been pregnant but had an abortion. Now her former husband, a star basketball player, was killing himself with drink. The parents of the boy were said to be distraught. They had to put their son in a sanatorium. Meanwhile, Paloma was running around with all sorts of men, and her father, the Minister of Defense, was not pleased.

"Paloma, won't you at least try to be a little more discreet?" he would shout, to no avail. Paloma merely laughed and tossed her mane of chestnut-colored hair. She was the only one in the world who was not afraid of her father. She had Spanish blood from her mother, and people said that accounted for her fiery temperament. But to look at her she was a rather plain wisp of a girl, with yellowish skin and dull eyes.

The Ortiz-Luizes were a powerful family. Willie Ortiz-Luiz had been the Minister of Defense for fifteen years. He controlled the army. All the funds budgeted for the military passed through his fingers. Several times before men had tried to kill him, but he escaped each time unscathed. He fortified himself behind the high stone walls of his mansion on Pili Road, now and then venturing out in an armored Mercedes, accompanied by two carloads of bodyguards. People let his children, Paloma and Jackie, do whatever they wanted. The sister and brother grew up thinking they were invincible.

They were wild children. Paloma had her men, Jackie had his guns. Their mother was a former beauty queen who had not been seen by anyone for years. People said that she had lost her mind, and spent her days hunting for lizards in the garden.

Jackie had already killed two men, each over some fancied slight—a chance remark, a badly timed snicker. The murders were efficiently handled by the Minister's people. There was never anything in the papers, only stories people handed down by word of mouth.

After they met, Bautista found that he was bumping into Paloma more often. Sometimes, while he was walking around a department store, she would run up, strangely breathless, an avid look in her gray-green eyes. Or, while in the swimming pool of the Manila Polo Club, he would see a dark shape darting through the water that turned out to be Paloma, coming up beside him and laughing at his surprise. Then she began dropping by the Stargazer and asking the waiters if they had seen him. She began calling him at his home. She told him she was bored, and needed someone to talk to.

When they began to date, he did not think much of it—not even when she took his hand, caressing the fingers, and pressing her thighs against his. He was used to having this kind of effect on women, and thought it was natural. Then her voice began to grate on him. She would not leave him alone. Soon, he lost all interest and began to treat her carelessly, as though she were a stray dog that had followed him up from the gutter.

He no longer read her letters, letters written on pale, scented sheets, filled with pressed flowers and schoolgirlish poetry. He was ashamed of sleeping with her. It happened one night after a party— he was drunk, and she was more than willing. She was feverish, almost wild, and he did not enjoy seeing her in his bed afterward. Even in sleep, her face retained a suggestion of tension, of insatiable hunger. He immediately got up and walked around the house, trying to clear his head of the fog that had settled over it.

The night he died, Bautista had not intended to go to a disco. He was at home, lying in bed, listening to the insistent whine of the mosquitoes against the wire-screened bedroom windows. He was thinking of Davao. He could see, with startling clarity, the old wooden house where his grandparents and his mother and father still lived. There was his mother, standing at the sink with her back framed by the kitchen door, washing dishes and pausing now and then to tuck a loose strand of graying hair behind her ear. There was his father, thin and stoop-shouldered, swatting at flies with his rolled-up newspaper. His grandfather and grandmother were in bed, sleeping. Their mouths were slack, a tear of saliva oozing out at the corners. They seemed almost to have stopped breathing.

Suddenly, Bautista felt afraid. He sat upright in the bed. The maids had forgotten to switch on the hall lights. He stared out the door, at blackness that was total and complete. He had the strange feeling that the rest of the house had disappeared, and that his room was floating in a void. He felt the heat like a living thing coiling around him. It clung to his arms, to his hands, to his brow, to the back of his neck. He decided to take a drive around the city.

Bautista drove aimlessly around the streets for a while. He noticed the look of misery on people's faces as they stood by the open doors and windows, fanning themselves. He shrugged when he saw flames shooting up into the dark sky from different corners of the city and heard the clang of the fire engines. The whole city was choking in the heat. He turned into Roxas Boulevard and headed for the Stargazer.

As he drove, the wind picked up and in a few minutes there was a low roll of thunder and the first fat drops of rain spattered against his windshield. By the time he reached the Holiday Inn, it was raining furiously. The hotel lobby had a cozy glow that warmed him and made him feel better. He entered the elevator and felt himself being borne swiftly upward—up and up, closer to the tangled constellations. When the elevator doors opened, he was happy. The loud music swept over him, the fumes of alcohol and cigarette smoke overpowered him and drew him forward. He gyrated with the crowd, at one with the writhing bodies. He sang along with the music, a song by Melissa Manchester that one heard everywhere in the city these days.

Outside the huge plate glass windows, the dark water of Manila Bay rushed up to the rocks of the breakwater and pulled back, rushed up and then pulled back. Farther out the water was very black and smooth, with only little ripples marring its surface.

The tap on his shoulder was light, and at first he did not turn. But it was repeated a few moments later, and his instinctive reaction was to jerk away from the intrusive touch. He turned and saw Paloma standing by his right shoulder.

"Hello, Bobby," Paloma said. She was smiling.

Bautista felt a hot anger grow inside him.

"Can't you leave me alone?" he said.

"Can't do it, Bobby," said Paloma, still smiling. She moved closer. "You're the one for me."

At that point, Bautista's hand rose. A gasp arose from someone watching, but Bautista did not hear it.

Paloma had not expected the blow and it caught her full on her right cheek. Her eyes widened. Her mouth was open—as though she wanted to say something—but no sound came out.

A dark figure began moving purposefully across the dance floor toward Bautista. People fell back at this figure's approach, as though seeing an apparition. But Bautista and Paloma remained standing close together. Perhaps they were both stunned by the enormity of what had just occurred. Paloma still had a hand on her cheek and Bautista stood quietly, with his head down. Those who were there said it looked like the last act of a badly rehearsed play, where the actors have to wait for someone to feed them their lines.

Bautista didn't live very long after that. The story of his suicide was in the papers the next day. They say General Vargas wrote that story. General Vargas was the army's Chief of Staff—a big, beefy man with dark, leathery skin and an ape-like face who swaggered about the city in army fatigues and combat boots, a pistol prominently displayed on his hip. Not ten minutes after the shooting, his men were at the disco and cordoned off the place. They kept everyone from leaving. The crowd of young boys and girls cowered and cried. They had no idea what was happening. The disco was too dark, the rock music too loud. They were dancing and enjoying themselves when the screaming and pandemonium began. People tumbled over chairs and tables to get to the elevators. Only a few got away; most were still there when General Vargas' men arrived in their army trucks. When the lights came on, they were puzzled by the dark, red bloodstains on the pink carpet where Bobby Bautista had died. The body itself was nowhere to be seen. Paloma was gone; she was already speeding home in one of her father's black limousines.

The General delivered a memorable speech, ordering all present to forget the events they had witnessed that night.

"Remembering only brings confusion," he said, "and amidst confusion all sorts of rumors arise. Please," he said, pausing for dramatic effect, looking at the audience as though they were a roomful of naughty children, "don't make my job any harder for me than it already is." He grinned. "Read about it in the papers tomorrow." His men took down the names of everyone there, and then let them go.

One or two people, the ones who had seen what had really happened, had difficulty falling asleep for weeks afterward. They kept seeing Bautista crawling to Jackie, pleading, "*Pare*, don't. I beg you, don't." He was sobbing and crying, clutching at Jackie's knees. But Jackie kept shooting. All in all, it took five shots to finish him off.

No one could have helped Bobby Bautista even if they had wanted to.

Overseas

Almost everyone in Manila has an uncle or a brother or even a father in Saudi Arabia. Since the government began exporting cheap labor there, long lines have formed in front of the Overseas Workers Bureau.

In Sepa's neighborhood only a few men remain—Sepa's father, *Mang* Pepe who runs the *sari-sari* store, and a few other men at whom the others laugh because, even though they want to go, their wives won't let them.

Everyone talks about the big money to be made in Saudi Arabia. *Mang* Kadyo, who just a year ago had been a jeepney driver like Sepa's father, now drives a bus in Riyadh. His wife, *Aling* Marta, says he earns more in one month there than he ever made in a year in Manila. Before, *Aling* Marta was always complaining about *Mang* Kadyo. She said he was lazy, that he was not a good provider. Her hands were always red and sore from washing other people's clothes in the big houses in Forbes Park. Now she stays home all day, listening to Sharon Cuneta tapes on a brand new cassette deck.

But a few men in the neighborhood have wives who don't care about the stories of big money coming back from abroad. Such wives only want their men with them, beside them every night. When a man goes to Saudi Arabia, it may be a year, even two, before his return trip home. Some wives simply cannot bear it. There is *Aling* Mameng, for instance, whose husband is very handsome, so one can understand why she can't bear to part with him. But then there is *Aling* Nena, whose husband looks like a laughing Buddha with a great big belly and spindly legs, and she is as jealous and possessive with him as though he were a Vic Vargas or an Eddie Garcia.

Even Sepa's older brother Rudy left. He had just turned eighteen. Before going to Saudi Arabia, he had sold Blue Seal cigarettes behind the Shell station on Pasay Road. She and Rudy used to sit on the bamboo ladder that led up to their house, telling funny stories and laughing and joking. Rudy bought her little trinkets from the money he had left over after he gave their father his share. If Sepa wanted a Coke from the *tiyanggi*, or money to see a movie, Rudy always gave her some. He was very good to her.

The day he told her, they were sitting on the bamboo ladder, watching the mosquitoes skim over the scummy green surface of the canal that ran beneath them. In the rainy season, this canal overflowed its banks and turned the neighborhood into a lagoon. Then Sepa would stay home from school and swim with the other children in the murky water. But now it was the middle of the dry season; the monsoon was a long way off.

She and Rudy sat on the steps and watched the smaller children standing ankle-deep in the water, catching tadpoles. There was a sickly sweet smell of rotting banana peels wafting over the canal from the far end, where piled-up garbage blocked the water's flow.

All the houses, including theirs, stood on stilts, with roofs made out of salvaged sheets of corrugated tin. The ground below was always muddy, even in the dry season, and sucked at the feet with every step. Under the houses lurked skinny bad-tempered cats with patchy fur. Some nights their wailing could be heard all over the neighborhood.

This time of year was so hot that the men walked around with their T-shirts up, exposing their beer bellies. And the women washing their clothes at the neighborhood pump wet their necks and shoulders, not minding how they looked in their soaked blouses. Sepa's loose blouse also clung to her back and shoulders and breasts, damp with perspiration. She lifted the ends of her blouse in both hands and tried to make the cloth flap. When her brother looked, she began to laugh.

At twelve, her breasts were just beginning to push up through her blouse. They were small, but the nipples looked enormous. She had been with a man once who told her that they looked like cauliflowers.

Sepa wondered if Rudy knew that she had begun seeing some of the young men and letting them buy her Cokes and treat her to movies. These young men always took her to the balcony and turned out not to be interested in the movies after all. But it was cool there in the dark of the movie house, and with the flickering image on the screen it was the closest Sepa had ever come to seeing the inside of a real disco, and so she didn't mind.

When she saw the look on Rudy's face, Sepa stopped laughing. "What's the matter?" she asked.

Rudy was silent for a few moments. Then he told her. "I've been thinking—maybe I'll sign up at the Overseas Workers Bureau." When she didn't answer, he continued, "Make a little money."

Sepa just looked at him. Rudy turned his back to her and began stretching, as though he'd gotten cramped from sitting too long.

Rudy was tall and dark and had big eyes. The women in the neighborhood found him handsome. He could have any girl that he wanted, but he was faithful to one, the daughter of *Mang* Tomas. She was only a few years older than Sepa and not even very pretty, but Sepa would see them sometimes, pressed up against each other in dark alleys or beneath stairs. Sometimes she would shout at them, "Hoy!" and they would both turn and look at her and laugh.

So she had thought her brother would not want to go to Saudi Arabia. It would be bad for her, too, to be left alone with her father at home. Sepa didn't have a mother—just someone who'd died of tuberculosis when she was four, and whose picture, encased in a plastic envelope, dangled from the rearview mirror of her father's jeepney. Her father was rarely home, and when he was she could smell him coming from a long way off, because of drink.

"Why do you have to go?" Sepa said. "We have enough money."

Her brother only shook his head.

"They want people to work in construction. You don't know anything about that," she continued. "And even if you're lucky enough to get there, you won't like it. You know how Boyet complains every time he comes home."

"I've made up my mind," Rudy said.

Sepa looked around helplessly. The neighborhood was so familiar that she had never stopped to look at it as a place other than home. She knew everyone in the surrounding houses, knew when they quarreled, knew when they made love. Surely that meant something. And no matter how ugly the place—yes, she already knew that the neighborhood *was* ugly—surely it was far better to be with people one knew, people one had grown up with, rather than with people who dressed strangely and spoke a language one could not understand.

She turned to her brother. "I didn't think you would be so selfish. How can you leave me alone with *Tatang*? All he does is drink, and he never gives me any money. He doesn't care about me."

"I'll send you money," Rudy said. "And you can always go to *Mang* Pepe or *Aling* Tancing if you need help. You won't be alone."

"I'll run away," Sepa said. "I will."

Rudy looked annoyed. "Stop talking crazy," he said.

Sepa merely shrugged.

Sepa thought she knew all she cared to know about Saudi Arabia from listening to the men talk at *Mang* Pepe's *sari-sari* store. In Saudi Arabia one couldn't have women and one couldn't have wine and the Filipinos were penned in at night, just like cattle, in a walled compound. Upon arrival, one had to sign a piece of paper, an agreement to turn over sixty percent of the pay to the Overseas Workers Bureau. Once a Filipino was caught stealing and instead of turning him over to the proper officials, the Saudis had cut off his right hand. The OWB officials there did not even bother to protest.

Sepa had the feeling that if her brother left she would not see him again for a long, long time.

"Don't leave," she begged, feeling near tears.

"I'll send you money every month," Rudy said.

Later, when Sepa told her father about Rudy's plan, she noticed he seemed pleased.

"Did he really say he was going?" her father said, rubbing his hands together. "That's good."

"He says he wants me to go to a proper school, to stop hanging around here with the older women," Sepa said, making a face. She never thought much about her future, about what was going to happen to her. That was why Rudy said she was stupid.

"With the money I send, you'll be able to have new clothes any time you feel like it, and you won't have to be ashamed to be with the other girls at school," Rudy said, guessing at the reason why she had stopped going. "You'll be happier. You won't have to depend on *Tatang* for things."

That last statement made Sepa stop and think. Perhaps Rudy was right. The money *would* be nice. There would be more to eat, for one thing—more than just the daily fare of *galunggong* and rice. And there might even be some money left over—after *Tatang* picked over his share, of course—for a small transistor radio, one she could carry around with her on the street. Then she could listen to Sharon and Martin and Pabs all day, without having to wait outside the local Disco-Rex to hear snatches of songs. And she could buy make-up, like the women she saw in the bars, who to her were the most beautiful women in the world, and who were always accompanied by pink-cheeked foreign men with plenty of money.

When the time came for Rudy to leave, Sepa was not as sad as she had expected to be.

"Write!" she begged.

"Sure!" Rudy said, smiling and giving her the "thumbs up" sign he imitated from an American tourist.

He was going on a big ship with many other men. He had described for her many times the route it would take. After leaving Manila, the boat would pass through the Strait of Malacca, cross the Indian Ocean, and head up the Red Sea to Jedda. At Jedda, the men would go different ways. Rudy was going to a city called Dharhan.

Dharhan. Sepa said the name over and over to herself. She imagined it to be a city in the middle of the desert, a city with sand-colored houses and buildings, where the tabletops might feel like sandpaper and even the food might have a gritty taste, the way it gets when cooked at the beach.

As Rudy prepared to go, Sepa thought he seemed sorry. He kept looking around, as though he were searching for something. There were a few people sitting out on the ladders of their houses: *Aling* Marta—picking the lice from the head of her eldest daughter; *Mang* Tomas, newly returned from Saudi Arabia, getting a haircut and a scolding from his wife, *Aling* Lita. They all stopped what they were doing to watch as Rudy made his way carefully down the ladder, all his belongings in a brand-new nylon bag, bought for the occasion by Sepa.

"*Oy*, Rudy, are you really leaving us?" *Aling* Marta said, punctuating the sentence with a loud guffaw.

"Yes, *Ale*, I'm leaving at last," Rudy said. "Look after Sepa, will you? I don't want her getting into any trouble."

Everyone laughed.

"Do you know when you're coming back?" *Aling* Lita said.

"Ay, don't expect to be back in less than two years," *Mang* Tomas sighed. "They try to get as much out of you as they can, while you're still fresh. Look at what they did to me..."

"Shussh!" *Aling* Lita said, boxing her husband's ear.

One by one, the neighbors from the various houses came to their windows and doors. A few of them waved. The air was full of warmth and good feeling. "Good-bye! Good-bye! May God be with you!" everyone was saying. Everyone was smiling, except for Rudy's girl, the eldest daughter of *Mang* Tomas. She was crying and blowing her nose into her skirt. In the last few weeks she and Rudy were always together in dark corners.

"*Stupida!*" her mother chided her. "Everyone has to leave sooner or later. Better that it was before you got pregnant!"

After that, Sepa didn't hear from her brother for a long, long time. The rainy season came and a few of the houses were blown down during a typhoon. But in a few days, they were up again with the occupants none the worse for wear. The canal overflowed its banks and the water rose halfway up the houses' stilts and for two weeks the girls had to walk with their skirts hitched up to their thighs to keep their clothes from getting wet. At night the wind howled through the narrow alleyways and the rain lashed the houses. The cats wailed like abandoned babies.

Sepa thought of her brother living in a city of adobe houses the color of the desert. Perhaps he had taken up with a Saudi girl. It made her happier to think so, to think that was the reason he had not written, though she knew it was unlikely—it was against the rules. When she passed the daughter of *Mang* Tomas on the street, the girl averted her eyes with an angry look. Once she even turned around and spat. Sepa shrugged. It was just one of those things.

Around the time of Typhoon Insiang—the typhoon that nearly knocked the figure of the Virgin from its pedestal in the tower of the Santuario de San Antonio—the old lady who sold fried bananas at a corner of the Avenida de Rizal had one of her periods of clairvoyance. She looked up at the grey sky and she noted the shapes of the clouds and she said the men were coming home. That was why, even before word got around that a few of the men from the neighborhood were going to be returning for a while, the wives had already begun their preparations—dusting and sweeping, putting up new curtains, buying new dresses. Vangie, the girl from El's Beauty Parlor, came several days a week to do perms. Sometimes she brought along a friend who did manicures.

Sepa was at the bus stop to greet the returning men, but her brother was not among those who stepped off the bus that had brought the men from the pier. There was *Mang* Enteng—darker and thinner than even she would have thought possible—and a few of the younger men, but no Rudy.

That night Sepa let someone take her to a movie, the first time in nearly a year. They sat in the darkened balcony a long time, and later the man did not want to take her home, because, he said, he hadn't had enough. Sepa went with him to a motel, and there they lay together in a bed which creaked and hurt Sepa's back. Afterwards, the man did not pay much attention to her. Sepa had hoped he might give her a little money, but he did not. When she returned home, her father was angry. He had waited for her to serve him his supper. He had to make do with leftover rice. He called her a slut and other bad names. Sepa stared at him impassively. "What's the use?" she was thinking. "It's all the same to me."

It must have been a few nights after that when the trouble between *Mang* Enteng and *Aling* Tancing started. People said later that they had seen it coming. *Aling* Tancing had acted a little crazy when her husband was away. The women whispered that she'd been taking tea made from bamboo roots. They said she'd been trying to lose something that was growing inside her, that perhaps was not her husband's. Then, just before her husband came home, someone saw her at the *herbolario* stand in front of Quiapo Church, buying little bottles filled with suspicious white powder. She said it was medicine to calm her nerves, a powder made from *camias* leaves. That was how matters were when *Mang* Enteng came home.

The first few days after his return, no one saw him leave his house. It was very quiet. So quiet that people began to talk about it over at the *sari-sari* store. The men began to exchange lewd jokes about what *Mang* Enteng was probably doing to *Aling* Tancing. Sepa, hearing this talk as she passed the store, would hurry on without looking up, folding her arms over her breasts and exhaling sharply, as if in anger.

She did not believe the stories about *Aling* Tancing, who was still young and always gave Sepa a little of the food she sold from a basket she carried on the top of her head—fertilized duckling eggs, mostly, but sometimes also fried banana and peanuts. *Aling* Tancing often looked very sad, but when she saw Sepa she brightened up and fussed over the girl's hair, combing back her bangs or arranging the ribbons Sepa liked to tie around her head. Perhaps it was because she alone of all the women in the neighborhood still did not have any children. *Mang* Enteng was much older than her, and they said he did not have much of his manhood left. Sometimes men would say what they would like to do to *Aling* Tancing if they had a chance. But all of this was just talk. Sepa knew that the men said these things about *Aling* Tancing out of boredom, out of not knowing what to do with themselves. Aside from such talk, there was really not much happening where they were.

Anyway, the thing happened on a night when there was a full moon. The old people say the full moon makes people a little crazy. On this night, everyone was outside because of the heat. And everyone heard the cries coming from *Mang* Enteng's house, and saw *Aling* Tancing running out, her nightgown torn from one shoulder, blood dripping from her nose.

"Help! Help! Enteng is trying to kill me!" she called out.

Mang Pepe took pity on her and let her in behind the counter of his store. She clung to him, sobbing. A few moments later, *Mang* Enteng himself appeared, shirtless, with a butcher's knife in his right hand.

"Where is she?" he shouted.

It looked as though *Mang* Enteng had become *huramentado*, and all the men ran away except for *Mang* Pepe.

Mang Pepe was not a very big man. It was on account of his slight build that he had not been accepted for a job at the Overseas Workers Bureau. Yet he spoke calmly to *Mang* Enteng, as though he never saw the butcher's knife.

"Now, what's all this about, *pare*?" he said.

"My wife has been cheating on me!" *Mang* Enteng cried.

At this, all the neighbors crept a little closer to their windows.

"Now now, now now," was all *Mang* Pepe could say.

"It's true! I can tell when my wife has been with other men.

She doesn't kiss the same!" Turning, he caught sight of *Aling* Tancing and pointed his knife at her. "You! Who used to be so modest! Now what makes you so hot? Learned a few things while I was away, ha?"

He made as if to leap over the counter. *Aling* Tancing screamed.

"Enteng! Enteng!" *Mang* Pepe was saying, holding him back. "If she had someone, don't you think the whole neighborhood would have known about it? And don't you think we, your friends, would have let you know? But Tancing is a good woman. She has never even so much as spoken to another man while you were away. Ask Sepa here, they are good friends and spend almost all their time together."

Mang Enteng glared distrustfully around, but Sepa was cowering behind a wall, trembling and shaking her head—no, no, no— as though her head were full of cotton, as though everything happening were just a bad dream. She was shaking and would not come out.

At any rate, *Mang* Enteng seemed to have been pacified. He lowered the knife and scratched his head. He began to look confused instead of angry.

"But how is it that she is so aggressive now?" he said to *Mang* Pepe. "Now it is so hard to satisfy her. Before, anything I did was all right with her."

Aling Tancing began to scream at him: "*Walang hiya ka*! Don't touch me! I am going back to Antique, to my mother's house!"

The people watching from their windows laughed. Then *Mang* Pepe took *Mang* Enteng aside and explained to him that it was because *Aling* Tancing loved him and missed him so much while he was away that she had nearly gone crazy from the strain and now behaved like a "low-flying woman."

"But—on top? On top?" *Mang* Enteng was heard to say.

Mang Pepe coughed discreetly. To Sepa, he seemed to have grown taller. She would look at him behind the counter and she would never be able to think of him in the same way again. "Go home now, Tancing," *Mang* Pepe said. "I'll walk home with Enteng later. You go on now."

Aling Tancing was ashamed of her condition. She did not look around at the people. She half-ran down the alley, and it was a week before anyone saw her again.

The first to visit her was Sepa. She brought some sweet rice cakes.

The two women sat on the floor of *Aling* Tancing's house, eating and having a good laugh at *Mang* Enteng's expense.

The first letter from Rudy came after the third typhoon of the year. The street was still littered with debris from the storm, but Sepa ran all the way home, the precious letter clutched tightly to her chest. That night, she read it aloud for her father by the light of the kerosene lamp.

The handwriting was bad, practically a scrawl. It said:

"My dearest *Tatang* and Sepa, forgive me for not writing for such a long time..."

He went on to explain that it had taken him a long time to adjust to conditions there. It had not been at all what he expected. The heat was dry and made him ill, and he had spent some time in a hospital. But he was back at work now, shoveling and loading bricks at the construction site for a new housing development just outside the city. It was hard work, he wrote, and he had to keep at it all day. Sometimes the heat went up to 110 degrees, and then he felt dizzy and nauseous but knew now what to do to keep from passing out. The other men had taught him how to drink scalding coffee and how to get by on just that all day. "Anything else," he wrote, "makes you sick to your stomach."

He wrote that he envied some of the others, like *Mang* Tomas, whom he'd heard was a driver of heavy equipment in Riyadh. "But they put me here because I'm big and I'm strong," he wrote. And there were worse jobs. A friend of his, a *Pampangueño*, had been assigned to do roofing work. After two weeks, he'd asked to be sent home. If the heat was 110 degrees on the ground, it was 135 degrees on the roof. "Enough to make one burst a blood vessel," he wrote. Hot tar had to be piped to the roof and spread out before they could lay the asbestos rolls, and his friend had burns on his back and arms from where the tar had burned right through his clothing. After a week, his hands had turned black and the stink of tar was always under his fingernails.

Other than the work, there was not really much to say about life in Saudi Arabia. One ate and then one slept. "My companions and I talk all the time about going home. And do you know? I have a longing to see the color green..."

The letter made Sepa very sad. She thought she could understand what Rudy must be feeling, out there in that other country with no rain, no greenery, perhaps even no sweet tastes. But her father—her father was angry.

"What? No money!" her father said.

He shook the envelope upside down, then poked around in it with his dirty forefinger. He opened the pages of the letter one by one, and then, when he realized that there really was nothing there, he flung the letter to the floor in disgust.

"*Tatang!*" Sepa cried, reproachfully.

"I'm going to the store," her father said, and went out.

Carefully, Sepa collected the scattered pages of her brother's letter. When she had them all neatly back in the envelope, she moved to the window. The rain had let up briefly. There was a fresh, clear scent from the trees that not even the stench from the canal could hide. The TV antennae that had sprouted in the neighborhood since the men started going to Saudi Arabia stood erect against the dark night sky.

The next day Sepa decided she was going to see the old lady, the clairvoyant. She had gone once before only the old woman had frightened her by probing her stomach with her long, bony fingers. The woman had told her about magic, how the force behind it resided in the will. Now this will was coiled up in her abdomen like a snake. It came not from the head, which was all reason, or from the heart, which was all emotion, but from the belly. It was like hunger.

Sepa closed her eyes and spread her hands over her belly. She thought she could feel something there, like a life force, stretching from her belly and becoming bigger and bigger. If she kept her eyes closed she could imagine this force growing so big it could swallow up whole oceans. She could not tell Rudy about what was inside her now—she knew it had something to do with the fact that her monthly blood had stopped. And now her whole body felt tender and bruised, her ankles and her wrists were swelling as if her feet and hands wanted to separate from the rest of her. She had caught *Aling* Tancing looking at her once or twice, looking at her with an expression of wonder and sadness in her dark eyes. *Aling* Tancing's own belly was as flat as a young girl's. Sepa had wondered at that—wondered why *Aling* Tancing could not grow anything inside her.

After a few moments, Sepa had to sit down. But she continued to think about Rudy, far away in Saudi Arabia. She thought he might be sleeping now, and she imagined him lying on a cot in a room filled with other men. She imagined herself entering the room and wandering among the silent, sleeping shapes, then stopping by one cot in the far corner. The figure was wrapped in a white blanket. She put her hand down softly on the blanket, and when the face was revealed, her brother smiled up at her.

Opportunity

Nina sat by the living room window, looking out at what was left of her mother's garden—the yellowing banana palms, the brown and patchy grass. She remembered when it looked different. She and her sister Celia were little, and there were rows of pink and yellow bougainvillea all along the garden walls. There were orange *gumamelas* by the front gate, and wasn't there, once, a coconut tree that her mother had made her father dig up because, she said, she was afraid a falling coconut might strike one of her children?

The late afternoon sunlight made everything look sepia-tinted, as in old photographs. Nina could see Mrs. Penaranda waddling down the street with her shopping bag bulging with fruit, but already she seemed like someone out of memory, as did the skinny, shirtless boys running around and around on the sidewalk in a game of *taya*. When Nina looked behind her at her parents, sitting close together on the flowered sofa in the living room, she suddenly saw an old, deaf man, blinking feebly in the dim light, and a woman with a perpetually angry look, rubbing a corner of her balled-up handkerchief between her right thumb and forefinger.

The old people's mouths and hands trembled. Nina wondered— was there a proper way to carry out a leavetaking? She was superstitious, after all. The day before, she had gone to mass and fixed her eyes intently on the young priest who was offering up the sacrament. His resplendent robes, white and purple, were a reminder that it was the season of Lent, of atonement. The electric lights were weak and flickered bravely in the gloom of the church, as though simulating candles. She felt the hard pew, cold beneath her knees, and silently urged the priest to intercede for her with Saint Jude, the patron saint of lost causes. Later, she had lit a votive candle at one of the side altars. Her small contribution rattled forlornly into the almost empty iron box. Yet she noted that nearly all the candles were lit. Now she would ask for her parents' blessing, though she knew they wouldn't give it.

"In a little while," she told them, "I'll send for you. Once I've gotten settled. Once I've found a job."

But her parents were silent. Nina wasn't sure they really understood. Her father had suffered a stroke not long ago. Since then it seemed to Nina that he grew tired of listening to people. He talked often of returning to his hometown of Bislig. Her mother, too, though younger and still capable, had a way of protecting herself by hearing only what she wanted to hear.

"I'm doing this for you," Nina continued. "You deserve an easier life."

"Are you going with—that man?" her mother said.

Nina looked at her. She nodded. Her mother turned her face away angrily and said, "What if he leaves you—when you are there?"

"He loves me," Nina said. The saying of it frightened her so much that she found herself trembling. She wanted her mother to say, "I understand." She wanted her mother to be kind.

Her mother had always been so belligerent, so quick to react to any slight. The wrong word elicited a slap, sometimes a beating. Even now that Nina was grown, she sometimes felt threatened by her mother's violence. Even now she could not be sure her mother would not hit her with her wooden slippers, as she had done so often when Nina was growing up.

"Please," Nina said softly. At that moment her mother leaned forward, into a slant of light from the window, and Nina could see clearly the patches of white hair at her temples, the fine skin mottled with light brown spots at the outer corners of her eyes. Her mother put her face close to Nina's, close enough for Nina to inhale the odor from her rotting gums, and said, "I know what will happen. He will leave you. When that happens, you will think about coming home. But you walk out that door, don't think you can come back."

Nina knew that her mother was thinking of what happened to Celia. Celia was only sixteen when she ran away with a man from Tanauan, a man her parents had met only once. He took Celia to live with his family in Batangas, and for a long time they did not hear from her. When they saw her again, she was standing at the front gate with her suitcases, looking thin and dark and worn-out, and later that night in the bedroom Nina had seen the large purple bruises on her sister's hips and thighs. Celia had simply shrugged and said that her husband drank. When Nina wanted to tell her parents, Celia had said impatiently, "Ah, stop that. Stop being such a baby."

Later, the man came to the house. He wanted to take Celia back to Batangas, but her mother would not allow it. She stood in front of Celia with her fists clenched and her mouth set in a hard line. Later, she even hit the man, raining blows about his head while the man stood silent, accepting her mother's blows with bowed head. Nina watched in terror from the stairwell. Her mother's hair had come loose from its bun and the long grey strands fell down her back, and Nina could see her mother's bare shoulder where her dress was starting to slip. She would have liked to hold her mother tight and still the flailing arms, but she had been afraid. Celia stood impassively, looking out the window as though the scene were not actually happening just a few feet away from her.

In the end, nothing happened. The man went away and in a few weeks Celia followed him, leaving her parents a note. Nina's mother screamed and pulled at her hair. Her sobs were deep and harsh and guttural, like the sounds an animal makes. For days she wandered around the house with her dresses only half-fastened, with her hair disheveled.

And Celia never came back to them. In bed at night in the room they once shared, Nina's eyes groped in the darkness, her ears strained for the familiar laughter. The silence was wounding, more wounding than the pain of her mother's fists on her mouth and shoulders. In the years that followed, any little thing was capable of setting her mother off. When Nina begged her mother to stop, her mother would say only that she hadn't hit Celia enough, and that was why Celia had turned out bad.

Nina wanted to tell her mother that if it were not for the memory of those beatings, Nina would put her arms around her, might even stroke her hair, which she had sometimes been tempted to do, but had never actually done in all her years of growing up. Now she could only stare at her mother's bowed head and wonder at how thick and long the hair still was, at how vigorously the gray-white strands sprang from roots. There was a strength in her mother like the strength of an ancient tree. Now the branches of this tree were so long and so far-reaching that if Nina did not back away, the tree would smother her.

Nina stood up, murmuring something about being late. Her father was stroking his wife's hair with trembling hands. Neither of them looked up as she slipped out the door.

Outside, it was a few moments before she could breathe properly again. She turned and tried to fix the house in her memory— the weather-beaten walls, green-tinged as though with fungi; the garden with its patchy grass, now overgrown with *talahib*. She thought about her parents, probably still huddled together in the living room—her father in a white shirt and the green-and-white striped pajamas he wore day in and day out; her mother, in a long-sleeved dress in spite of the heat, clutching her rosary beads. She told herself, they will manage. There was the chicken farm, of course, though that had not been doing too well lately. It was a small farm, only a few hundred chickens. There had been troubles—chicks disappearing, electric wire stolen—and her father had taken to sleeping there, in the back seat of his old Volkswagen Beetle because they had still not saved enough to build a modest resthouse. Her mother took the bus there early in the morning to bring her husband food, and usually returned close to midnight, her ankles swollen from walking.

Nina could not bear to be on the farm, with the ever-present flies. The relatives called Nina ungrateful. They said she was *walang hiya*. They said what a shame it was, that a girl with a university education did not even help her parents out. The last time she had gone with her parents to the farm, the heat and the ever-present flies made her ill. Her parents took her to a small lake, and they rested there while she drank some cool coconut juice and tried to collect herself. Nina tried to focus on the mountain on the other side of the lake, which rose from the water, blue and perfect. The water of the lake was very still, and in it she saw reflections of the *bancas* and the clouds. Later her father sent someone to bring them food. There was warm rice, wrapped in banana leaves, and fish. She saw her father laugh like a much younger man when Nina's mother tried to feed him some sweet rice cakes. She saw her mother dip two fingers into the water of the lake and bring it to her lips. Her parents acted like they were behaving for Nina's benefit. Nina only looked away, wanting to get back home as soon as possible. On the long ride home, in a corner of the back seat, Nina had curled up and tried to keep from inhaling the dust coming in through the open car windows. Nina never accepted another invitation from her parents to go with them to the farm.

Tony told her that he felt her parents were wasting their time. "Why can't they get someone else to manage the farm for them?" he said. Nina shrugged helplessly.

Tony was a much older man. She met him through an advertisement in *The Philippine Star*. Daily, she and a girlfriend would peruse the want ad columns for likely prospects. There were always a few Australians, Europeans, and Americans looking for Filipina companions. They had heard that Filipinas were very gentle, affectionate, and easy to please. They always asked for a picture.

Nina's girlfriend had received many offers and debated whether to choose between a Japanese or an American. "Japanese men expect their wives to walk behind. American men wash their own dishes," was how she explained her final decision.

When Nina received Tony's first letter, she was almost too happy. Until then she worried that she was too dark, not *mestiza* enough. Her eyes were what they call *singkit*—small and chinky. Before going to have her picture taken at the Foto-Time machine outside Shoemart Department Store, she tried to correct these flaws with make-up, applying beige powder to her face and neck, drawing two dark lines down either side of her nose with brown eyeshadow, smudging black eye-pencil around her eyes. She was careful, in the picture, not to reveal her arms, for the difference in skin tone would have been immediately apparent. And yet, this American had singled her out! For a year, she carried his letters around with her in her handbag, stopping at street corners to read them over.

"Dearest Nina," he wrote, "what a lovely name you have! I would like very much to meet you in person..."

Then he made arrangements to come to Manila. Nina advised him to wait until July, when it would be cooler because of the rains. He agreed. In the meantime, he sent her pictures of his three-bedroom house in San Bruno, a small community just south of San Francisco, and of his three children by a former wife. Nina had not known, until then, that he had once been married. But he wrote her that it had happened when he was very young, barely out of his teens, and that he had been impulsive. He wrote that the experience made him want a calm, rational relationship with a quiet woman.

As for the house, it stood on the side of a steep hill, and on either side were houses that looked exactly like it. There was a small front lawn smoothly carpeted with grass, and two cars side by side on the driveway.

It was around this time that Nina began to dream. She dreamt that she was already in America. In her dreams, she was always cold, and always standing outside the house. She could hear a child's laughter in the background. She was disturbed because her parents seemed to have no place in this dream. She tried sometimes to imagine them standing at the front window of the house, looking out, but always their faces seemed so still and so unmoving that they reminded Nina of puppets. Then Nina became so frightened that she would begin to cry, and soon afterwards she would wake up feeling anxious and depressed.

Her first meeting with Tony had been in the Aristocrat restaurant on Roxas Boulevard. He looked older than he had in the pictures. His hair was completely white, and the skin around his neck and jaw was loose and wrinkled. She guessed he must be close to sixty. From the first, he had a way of looking at her that was very direct and made her turn her face away in confusion. Right there in the restaurant he bent down and kissed her full on the lips. She immediately glanced around and saw a few matrons shaking their heads and puckering their lips. For some reason, Celia's words came to her just then: Ah, stop that. Stop being such a baby. After that, she was able to toss her head proudly and ignore the looks from the other tables.

Tony had said he would take care of the visas and the papers. He had a friend in the American Embassy who could help them. She would have to take a jeepney to Buendia and from there catch a bus that would bring her to M.H. del Pilar, to the Hotel Aureliano II, where Tony was waiting. He had bought the plane tickets only the day before. For days she wavered, not sure that she was doing the right thing. She cried, she said she couldn't leave, then she made up her mind suddenly, in a kind of cold determination.

Now she would be late, and she could imagine Tony pacing back and forth in his room, checking his watch repeatedly.

Near the intersection of Santolan and Camias, she managed to flag down a jeepney. It was one of the more ornate ones, with flashing mirrors and a spray of gaudy flowers painted on the hood. A sign above the windshield proclaimed, in flowing, red script: *REBELDE*. The driver paused only long enough for her to put her right foot on the lowest step. She swayed unsteadily as the jeepney lurched forward, but managed to duck into the narrow space where two rows of people sat facing each other on low benches.

It was dark in the cramped, narrow space, and at first Nina imagined that it must be full. But a fat matron with a bulging shopping bag who was sitting farther in called out, "*Ale!*" and gestured to a few inches of space that had suddenly materialized between her and a gaunt, sour-faced man in a dirty, white T-shirt.

Nina staggered forward. She was immediately engulfed by the smell of onions from the lady's shopping bag and the smell of sweat from the sour-faced man. But it was not, curiously, an unpleasant experience. She was comfortable sitting with one elbow buried somewhere in the matron's side, the other pressing against the man's ribs beneath his T-shirt, her knees knocking against those of another man across the aisle, who continually smiled and nodded as though he wanted to make her acquaintance.

The closeness, the smells, the unlooked-for familiarity seemed to buoy her up. She felt as she often did at the beach when, floating on her back, she allowed the warm water lapping at her skin to carry her now here, now there, lulling her into a stupor. She liked the darkness and the proximity of so many bodies, and was sorry only that she could not see more of the city from the chinks between the people's heads and shoulders. She thought she saw a few low, weather-beaten buildings, and dusty storefronts advertising Coca-Cola and Seven-Up, but then the jeepney hit a particularly bad stretch of road, and everything jerked so much that the landscape blurred and became an indistinct jumble of reds and yellows.

It was nearly dark when she reached the Hotel Aureliano II, a shabby, cockroach-infested building at the end of a narrow side-street. Tony's room was on the fourth floor. The one window looked out on a narrow courtyard, enclosed on three sides by buildings and on a fourth by the street. She had come to know every particular of that room, and especially the configurations of the cracked plaster on the ceiling.

The bed was noisy. She knew how it would be—Tony would thunder and shove while she lay very still, listening to the echo of springs from the next room. She knew that a Japanese businessman had the room to the left, and a Swedish tourist the room to the right. One night she heard loud, banging noises coming from the Japanese's room and thought—though Tony told her she was imagining this—she heard the sound of a girl's whimper. The next morning, she passed the Japanese in the hallway and shrank against the wall. But the man only nodded politely and barely glanced at her.

As she entered the lobby through the revolving doors, she saw the bell boys stare and it seemed to her that one or two were beginning to snicker. She thought she heard them whisper, as she walked with flaming cheeks to the elevator, *puta*, whore.

But she was elated. The thought of the life that was to come filled her with exaltation. She thought of Tony, waiting for her in the room. Washed and shaven, with his hair meticulously blow-dried, he would look as he did when she first met him—immaculate in white pants, white shoes and a carefully pressed, light blue sports shirt. She laughed, thinking of how they would look, standing together before an immigration official in San Francisco: she and her sixty-year-old American boyfriend with the blow-dried hair and the immaculate appearance. Her own hair was now stiff with dust and dried-up perspiration. Her face needed washing. She imagined an immigration official staring at her and shaking his head. The official would not want to admit her but Tony would show him the papers. He would do this with a flourish, the way she had seen it done in the movies.

"It's all perfectly legal," Tony would say, in that sarcastic voice of his.

The official would turn red. "Yes, of course," he would say. To her he would add, "Welcome to America."

And she would walk proudly on, hardly deigning to glance at him.

Yes, she thought. Let the man have what he wants now. She jabbed at the elevator button with anxious fingers. "Take me," she whispered. "Please, please take me."

God's Will

I hear my father again. His room is on the other side of this wall, his bed pressed up against it so I can tell from the creaking of the bed springs when he is having a bad night.

My wife Teresa and I lie awake in the darkness, listening. Neither of us speaks. No matter how tired we are, we always wake at the slightest sound. Tonight my father is weeping.

I get up and go into my father's room. He is sitting up in bed, saying over and over: "I'm afraid." I take him in my arms. I tell him to stop. But he will not stop. So then I try to shame him: "Is this how a del Pilar behaves?" All his life he was formal and dignified, and even though my mother said he was lazy and not a good provider, at least he had his pride.

When he was a young man, he was very handsome. He used to walk in the Luneta in a neatly pressed *Americana*, a Panama hat on his head and an ivory-handled cane in his right hand. How my mother swooned at the sight of him! She and her classmates at La Consolación College were all mad about him. When he married my mother, the girls used to tease her about the big fish she had caught. They used to pinch her arms until she was black and blue. "Uy, Choleng, you sly one!" they would say. "Tell us how you did it."

I look at my father now and note how his belly spreads over his belt. His jowls have sagged and his eyes have a disappointed look. Over the years he seems to have lost his capacity for life.

He sits by the window, looking bored and irritable. His hand gropes absent-mindedly in the bowl of sunflower seeds my wife thoughtfully placed on the coffee table beside him. Mechanically he munches, without once looking away from the window. His eyes are vacant, and his mouth seems to function purely from habit, a habit of chewing and swallowing. This is how he spends whole afternoons.

If I try and talk to him, he gives me a blank look, his eyes like two gray stones. His hand is limp. I take it between my own, and again am amazed by its softness—the hand of a man who never had to lift anything in his life.

I ask him: Would you like to go for a drive? Would you like to have *merienda* out?

He only withdraws his hand from mine and turns again to look, impassively, out the window.

Last year, my mother died. She was eleven years younger than my father, only seventy-two. She died very suddenly in her sleep. No one knows why. Her yearly check-ups were always fine—no symptoms. Dr. Fontanilla said she was as healthy as a *carabao*. Afterwards, Dr. Fontanilla could say only that it was most probably her nerves. He said that as long as he had known Choleng, she had always been a nervous woman.

In the months before her death, she grew much thinner. My wife and I became accustomed to a new shrillness in her voice when she spoke to my father. At night we heard them arguing, their voices rising and falling, rising and falling, from the other side of the bedroom wall. After a while, we no longer bothered to listen. Their voices were like the noise of a train passing, or like the noise of traffic from the nearby highway. When my mother died, we found out we couldn't get used to the silence. We sat up all night listening to the croaking of the frogs.

There are times now when I find myself standing in the middle of a room, not knowing what I am doing there. My hand, poised to reach for something, forgets what it is after in mid-grasp.

I put away the wedding pictures—those pictures from a long-ago time showing my mother with her eyebrows black, black in her pale, round, laughing face; her hair piled high on top of her head like some strange architectural creation; her tiny waist; her shoes, silver and satin, with cloth flowers near the tip. I put them away because I could not bear to see, standing beside her, the picture of my father, resplendent in his expensive tuxedo, his eyes round and vacant, his face placid, his hands limp on my mother's shoulders.

My wife says my mother is still with us. Once I heard my wife calling, and when I came up she pointed to a white moth clinging obstinately to a sheet she had hung out to dry. "Choleng," she whispered with a solemn air. I took her hand, unable to speak.

I agree that my mother is still with us. How else to explain what happened the other night? I fell asleep exhausted on the living room sofa. Later, I woke and saw a dim shape sleeping on the other sofa across from me. I thought it was my wife and, thus reassured, fell back asleep. I dreamt then of my mother. She was all in white and there was a strange bright light shining behind her. She seemed happy in that other place. At least her face had an expression that was not sad, not quite the look she had when she was alive.

I dreamt that she held something in her arms. "Shhh, Shhh," she whispered as I approached. I saw that it was a meringue. I had never seen one so huge. She cradled it in her arms like a child's head. It was streaked with brown near the tip. She held it out to me, like an offering. She was smiling. I was about to take it from her when bright red blood suddenly trickled down her nose. I woke up then, my heart pounding. I could still see my mother's pale face, and the blood running from her nose. My wife looked sleepily up from the bed in our room. "Weren't you downstairs with me last night?" I asked. She shook her head. "But I saw you—you were sleeping on the sofa across from me," I insisted. Then my wife got up and took my hand. "Do you think it's possible—?" she said, looking carefully at me. I nodded, and before I could actually utter the words, the words that were in my heart, she whispered: "Choleng was here."

My mother's friends come by now and then to check on my father. They all have the same stories of woe to tell. There are a few interesting variations, but for the most part their stories are all about someone contracting an incurable illness, or someone dying.

The latest visitor, *Nang* Piyang, told a story about one of her nephews—a very young man, only twenty years old, he was on the Korean Airlines jet that had been shot down over Siberia by the Russians. I looked at *Nang* Piyang, not sure whether she was making it up. She is almost as old as my father, but unlike him, is still active—gardening, cooking, and playing mahjongg in the afternoons with her cronies. Her hair is permed and this afternoon she has powdered her face and applied lipstick. I believe her story, in spite of myself.

Nang Piyang said the boy might have taken another flight, but his mother was in a hurry for him to get back. I looked at my father. His expression never changed.

"How terrible," my wife said, her eyes filling with tears.

"Humph," was all my father said. He confined himself mostly to stuffing his mouth with boiled peanuts.

After *Nang* Piyang left, my father took a napkin and carefully wiped off the chair where she sat, as though she might have brought a disease into the house. I became angry and asked him what he thought he was doing. He merely gave me a cold look and went to his room.

In bed that night, I mentioned this strange behavior to my wife. She sighed and said, "*Tatang* was meant to live a very long time"— which meant that my father is one of those lucky people who bring grief to others, but never to themselves.

It is true. I still remember how terrible his bath times were, both for my mother and myself, who had to watch. How Choleng struggled to lift his inert mass from his wheelchair into the bathtub! He was almost twice her size, yet his pride prevented him from allowing anyone else to help him. And how my mother used to scrub that stubborn, inert flesh, that had darkened and toughened over the years, and was impervious to any of her ministrations.

If anyone were to ask, I would say that Choleng died of exhaustion, sheer exhaustion.

At times when I am most discouraged, I ask my wife, "What should I do?" She brings me white powder pounded from *camias* leaves. She brings me bamboo roots to mix with my tea.

"This will cure your nerves," she says. "That's all it is—just nerves. You inherited it from your mother."

Now I stay at the office as late as possible. On the way home I stop by the *Santuario*, though I am not a religious man. I sit on a bench close to the altar, where I can gaze on the peaceful faces of the saints, all pink-cheeked and red-lipped, in their brocaded robes. One or two people are making the rounds of the Stations of the Cross. Otherwise, it is very quiet and dark.

I like to listen to the priest recite vespers in his sonorous voice,

and I like the smell of the incense as it wafts from the brass cen-
ser he swings three times at points during the service. I have
sometimes thought of talking to this priest, and telling him about
my problems with my father and with my wife. He is a big, burly
Spaniard, Father Hugo, with a loud voice that booms through the
church during sermons, making it impossible to sleep.

I imagine myself telling Father Hugo about my father. Perhaps
it will be during the weekly confession, and in the darkness of the
cubicle I can see only the outline of Father Hugo's bowed head
on the other side of the screen. "I blame him," I say to Father Hugo.
"He caused my mother's death." Father Hugo absolves me in the
same beautiful tenor voice with which he leads the church choir.

I sense my father's wakefulness—I can hear his bedsprings
creaking, first on one side and then on the other. The bed is too
big, the sound of a solitary person moving around on it somehow
not right. It is a large four-poster, made of fine, dark mahogany—
the same bed my parents slept in on their wedding night. When
we moved from Panay, my mother wanted it shipped to Manila. I
protested, but she would not listen. It was brought by boat, and
four workmen hauled it up the stairs and into their room. In the
process the workmen knocked against the walls and the scrape marks
are still there.

I can hear the old man's breathing, and Teresa's, too. One breathes
noisily through his throat, and the other softly and gently, as though
sighing. The two sounds intermingle and I can no longer tell who
is beside me or which room I am in. Locusts whir in the garden.
Frogs croak from the pond. A breeze whispers through the branches
of the lychee tree outside the window. I am drifting into sleep when
I imagine a figure lying next to my father in the old bed. Then,
darkness.

The next day my father is sitting by the window again. I glance
gloomily in his direction, and notice for the first time that his head
is misshapen—one side looks larger than the other. Old women
say that when a baby is newly born, the skull is very soft. If one
doesn't turn the head properly, from side to side, one side gets
flatter than the other and it affects the brain. I become agitated
and look around to tell my wife. But my father is beckoning. He
has a look I sometimes see on the face of the washerwoman when
she is about to deliver a piece of lewd gossip—seeing it on my father frightens me so much I hesitate.

Marianne Villanueva

"Pssst!" he says, impatiently.

"What is it?" I ask.

"Come closer, come closer," he says. When I am close enough, he rests his fist clumsily at the back of my neck, forcing my head down. In my ear he says, "I am going to tell you a secret. Don't tell Teresa! I have a *nobya*."

My heart constricts. Teresa is watching. She has put down the book she is reading and looks at me with a strange expression.

My father continues, pointing to the far corner of the garden, "Do you see that banana palm over there?" The tree he points to is stunted and small, a relic of the days when Choleng used to care for the garden. Its yellowing leaves stand out against the dark green of the moss-grown wall. "Everyday she stands there and waves at me."

I look at the garden but, of course, it is empty. Stupid, I chide myself. Did I really expect to see someone there? Our garden walls are at least six feet high, and on top there are coils of barbed wire and shards of broken glass to keep intruders away. But there is something in my father's face, in the intensity of his grip on my shoulder.

"Yes," I say finally.

"Isn't she beautiful?" my father whispers.

"Yes, she is beautiful," I say, and this seems to satisfy the old man. His grip relaxes, and a look of contentment appears on his face.

That night, I go out to the garden. I stand next to the banana palm that my father gazes at so intently. There is a strong wind. The branches of the trees rustle and sway. At that moment, I have the feeling that the garden itself is alive and is speaking to me, a feeling that the murmurings of the leaves are a language. I listen closely. After standing and listening a long while, I think I can differentiate between what individual plants and bushes are saying. The lychee tree whispers, "Don't fret, don't fret." The magnolia tree murmurs, "Trust, trust, trust." I feel roots rearranging themselves in the earth beneath my feet. Then, my mother is there. I cannot see her but I can hear her voice, unmistakable. It comes from the heart of the trees, where the sap and the root and the life of the world come together. "God's will," she says. "What?" I say, as though bewitched. "Speak louder."

"Trust in God's will," she says.

Now the banana palm shivers—a sudden breeze. I feel cold and the garden seems a dangerous place, full of shadows. I make my way back to the house. My wife is there, kneeling at my father's feet. She has his two hands in hers, and is looking up at his face with an expression of tenderness. The old man looks down at her, and then he lifts one of his hands to stroke her hair.

"*Iha*," my father says. "Thank you, *iha*."

My wife is holding my father's urine bottle, which I see now is full. She must just have finished helping him. In the beginning, I was happy that she was not the kind of woman who shied away from such things. Perhaps from so many years of watching my mother, such things have come to seem natural to her.

It occurs to me to ask: who is it who has been bathing my father since my mother died? I picture my wife assisting my father in and out of the tub. I imagine his heavy weight on her thin shoulders. I see the daily struggle in the bathroom with a clarity that dumbfounds me.

I step forward, and my wife turns. But she remains where she is. My father only looks contemptuously at me and shuts his mouth tight.

I go up to the bedroom and lock the door and sit with my head in my hands. I tell myself: he is just an old man. But then I remember his face, and his look of satisfaction when he spoke of his *nobya*: "Isn't she beautiful?" Then I am filled with such revulsion that I have to restrain myself from throwing him out of the house altogether.

That night, I can't sleep. I lie awake, long after I hear my wife's breathing settle into its familiar rhythm. I find myself straining to hear my father on the other side of the wall. He was unnaturally silent at dinner, only staring down at his plate and not even bothering to eat the tamarind-flavored soup my wife prepared. He seemed anxious to go to bed. I helped him up, helped him get undressed. Then I helped him prop the pillows around his head. Since then, not a sound. His room is silent. The silence is oppressive. It is a silence that reminds me of cellars and other dank, enclosed spaces. I cannot even hear the crickets tonight. The silence is vast and deep and large—as large as the night. Finally, I get up and listen at his door. I knock. No answer. I know he is awake. I can feel his anger and resentment through the door. I say, "*Tatang*? *Tatang*?" Still no answer. Finally I creep back to bed and wrap the blanket tight around my wife and me.

The Special Research Project

The building was old. How old exactly, no one was certain. The records of the construction were lost in the great fire that struck Manila in 1915. Judging from the style of its architecture and its ancient, weather-beaten look, however, it had been built at the turn of the century.

This was the building that housed the National Archives. The shelves were full of dusty, yellowing documents from Spanish times, newspapers with courageous names like *La Independencia* and *La Solidaridad*, and books on history and geography compiled by the Spanish friars. No one had looked at the books for a very long time. They were piled together in haphazard fashion on the shelves. The pages were coming loose from the bindings. The newspapers were slowly crumbling to pieces. Perhaps the past was not very important, or perhaps no one wanted to remember that before the New Society of the dictator Roberto Suarez Gomez, there had been such a thing as an intellectual life in the country. At any rate, the building's long, narrow corridors were empty. Nothing disturbed the shafts of sunlight slanting quietly through the high windows.

So many years had gone by, years in which the building had gradually passed into crumbling decay, that the Ministry of Buildings and Construction condemned it as unsafe. A team of workers was dispatched to begin the demolition. The workers might never have found the old man if they had not decided to first examine the building from top to bottom, climbing stairs hidden in dark corners and trying doors that had never been tried. He would have died there with his books, his bones crushed amid falling stone and metal, and no one would ever have known why he shut himself up in a windowless cubicle at the very top of the building for twenty-odd years.

When the workers found him, he was already very old. He had lived away from the light for so long, in a world of books and deep silence, that he had almost forgotten how to speak. He waggled his hands uselessly in distress at the workers' coming, at the sound of their intrusive voices and their heavy, thumping feet. When they told him he had to leave, he cried like a child, the tears sprinkling the collar of his shirt. At last they realized that he had been happy living there, and that the outside world terrified him.

He was sitting at a massive, wooden writing desk with a sheaf of loosely bound manuscripts and a stack of writing paper pushed to one side. All around him, on the walls and floor, were books of all sizes and descriptions. Filipino writers and historians, long gone, stared solemnly up from dusty book jackets. Jose Rizal, Marcelo H. del Pilar, Francisco Balagtas, Horatio de la Costa, Salvador P. Lopez. They were names no one had ever heard of, yet reading them now gave the workers a strange sense of loss. It was as though they were suffering from collective amnesia. They could not imagine what life must have been like in the old days, when books were prized and writing was an honorable occupation.

From the half-finished manuscripts and other writing paraphernalia on his desk, they guessed the old man was a writer. But they could not understand what he had to write about in his dreary surroundings. They said to themselves that he must have been a crank and they led him away, while he thrashed his arms and babbled incoherently about "a project." They brought him to the district captain—a leering, uneducated man—and that night he slept on a hard pallet in a home for vagrants where his cries went unheard by the grim-faced wardens.

Later, the man who had been instructed to clear out the room made an interesting discovery. In one of the old man's desk drawers he found a document with the strange title: "The President's Special Research Project." The paper was speckled with cockroach droppings, and the slightest breath upon a page shook up a cloud of dust. Yet in one corner of the document was the faint outline of the Presidential seal.

The old man, whose name, if anyone had cared to ask, was Nicanor, had kept the document in the drawer for many years. In the beginning he used to take it out and look at it from time to time. But he already knew most of it by heart, and toward the end he did not like to move it because of the fragility of the paper. Therefore he left it in the desk drawer, and no one else remembered when it was written, or why, and the document was placed in a plastic bag along with the books and other paraphernalia, for later disposal.

The Project grew out of a dictator's obsession with history.

In the early years of his reign a young and handsome Gomez looked out over the green and gold rice fields and felt the first stirrings of a need for immortality. He had just spent five years leading his armies from the Ilocos provinces in the far north to Albay in the south, from the heights of Benguet province to the lowlands of central Luzon. With bullets he had flayed the Lopez and Vargas families and made himself the new master of mountains and plains. Only thirty-five, he had an old man's eyes. He wanted to go down in history as the greatest President the Philippines had ever known. He wanted to be greater even than that old Spanish patrician, Quezon, who guided the country through the turbulent first half of the century. Therefore it was only natural that he should desire to leave a written record, a personal chronicle, of his reign.

Over the years, the idea grew into a magnificent obsession. A search began for the man who would undertake the President's Special Research Project. From Batanes in the north to Mindanao in the south, anyone who had ever written anything—a poem, a short story, a play—was forced to surrender the manuscript for inspection by a special panel of judges who would decide whether the applicant had the necessary literary flair, feel for history, and political allegiance required by such a project.

Finally, it was announced in the papers that the search was over, and nothing more was heard about the President's Special Research Project for a very long time.

Then books began to appear with the dictator's name, books describing his accomplishments. These books were found in all the bookstores, and were required reading in all the classrooms. They all had the same quotation on the frontispiece, from the President himself:

> I set these words down *so that in the future my greatness*
> *be known and my words believed by men.*

Every few months another book appeared. There were so many that they began to take up whole sections in the libraries. They were very beautiful books, with hard covers and shiny paper, blinding white, that people whispered had been imported from Japan. They made the books on the other shelves look even more shabby than they really were—the books written on brown paper from recycled newspapers, with such tiny print one needed a magnifying glass to read. People were not used to such beautiful books and approached the shelves very reluctantly, with the same hesitation they felt at going down the main aisle of the church in the middle of the service. Librarians pointed out these books to visitors with great pride. "We have such an educated President," they would say.

But a curious thing happened. People began to actually question whether the President had written these books. How could he know so much about the history of the Philippines—he, who had never even attended college, who was whispered to be the illegitimate son of a general and a maid? And it was curious, too, how the books would appear so regularly, even though various crises arose in the government that demanded all of the President's time and attention—like the tidal wave that destroyed Cavite, and the secessionist struggles in Mindanao.

Those who believed the President had actually written the books said that he probably stayed up late at night, when everyone else had gone to bed and it was quiet.

"He is a very deep man, a truly brilliant man," these people all said. "He is different from the others who came before. He is the first one to care about our history."

The ghostwriter did not lead an unpleasant life. He was alone, but he liked the solitude. It was very quiet there, on the top floor of the National Archives. No one knew he was there; the creaky old elevator reached only to the floor below. His door was unmarked, and in any case he always kept it locked. He did not like visitors. Not that he expected any. Even the few Presidential aides who knew about the Project did not like going to the National Archives.

Nicanor delivered the manuscripts himself to the President. This entailed his leaving the National Archives once a week and making his way through the crowded streets to Malacanang Palace. To someone so used to the solitude of the archives, the trip—seated in an old bus that choked and lurched at every pothole, surrounded by anonymous bodies that reeked of perspiration—was a disagreeable experience, something to be endured. When he finally arrived at the Palace, a guard ushered him in through a service entrance. Then he found himself in the "dirty kitchen"—that is, the place where chickens were gutted and cleaned, and pots and pans scrubbed. It was a place of general hubbub and disorder, a noisy place. Nicanor was forced to stop up his ears as he passed through here, and the servants pointed to him and laughed—that strange old man, always rushing through with a bundle of papers under his arm.

When he had made it past the kitchen, Nicanor found himself in the basement of the Palace. From here he would have to traverse long corridors, and go up one flight of stairs after another to reach the main offices of the President and his staff. The rugs here were rather threadbare. The corridors were narrow, and the white walls had scuff marks where careless movers had knocked furniture against the walls.

Finally, he came to an open door leading into an empty room. The room had an expectant air: there was a sofa and, directly opposite, a desk and a heavy *narra* armchair. Nicanor sat on the sofa and waited. While waiting, he looked about—not nervously, because he had been here too many times—but curiously, as if to see whether there were any further deterioration in the physical surroundings since his last visit, the previous week. Sometimes he found cigarette butts on the floor. Sometimes he noticed dust on the red brocade curtains that framed the wide windows. The ring marks from the President's water glass were still on the desk.

The President entered through a door at the far side of the room. He always wore a neatly pressed *barong Tagalog* with two panels of intricate embroidery down the front, and a pair of mother-of-pearl cufflinks. His hair was neatly combed and slicked back with *pomada*. He had undoubtedly stayed up late the night before, yet he appeared alert and energetic, and briskly picked up the manuscript that Nicanor had placed on the desk.

He was not a very tall man. When he addressed the *masa* from the balcony of his Palace, he had the habit of raising both arms heavenward as he spoke, as though invoking divine guidance. His strong voice had a sonorous, hypnotic quality. The crowd standing below listened as if mesmerized, though afterward no one could recall what the President had actually said.

"But he looked splendid!" the people always exclaimed. "So handsome!"

The President sat very quietly, looking over the pages, not making a sound. At certain points, his brow furrowed, as though he was displeased. But he remained silent. Finally, he put the pages down. Perhaps he had read enough. Perhaps he didn't like the way Nicanor was looking at him from the sofa. Perhaps he was only pretending to read. At any rate, he got up to go. He always extended a hand to Nicanor and said, "Good work," with an air of slight condescension. Then Nicanor picked up his things. He was confused because the President said nothing about a chapter that Nicanor had worked on over and over, a chapter that described the President's boyhood.

It was difficult for anyone to imagine that the President had a childhood. The people had grown so used to thinking of him as the great general, the conquering hero. The papers gave the impression that the past was not very important—that before Gomez had become president there had been no real history. It had come to seem entirely possible that Gomez had sprung full-grown from his mother's womb. For that matter, it was even possible to believe he could walk on air.

Yet Nicanor had discovered the President's childhood, as though it were a lost country to which he alone had the key. The childhood had been lurking behind the President's desk in his room at the Palace, and on one of Nicanor's visits he had seen its shadow by his right foot. Before the President had time to notice what he was about, Nicanor had very carefully retrieved the childhood and put it in his pocket. He carried it back with him to the National Archives and let it go. Then the childhood roamed the dusty corridors, delighting in the old books and in the stacks of writing paper. It told Nicanor stories of that long-ago time when it had not been a prisoner in the Palace, and Nicanor could hardly restrain his excitement. He wrote it all down, and the scenes that he wrote now were so delicately drawn, so intricate in their particularity of detail, that he was sure anyone reading would say, "Yes, this is how it was—exactly how it was."

Here was Gomez, swiping caramel tarts from the neighborhood grocer and trading insults with the shirtless vendors hawking *tsampoy* and *titina* along the streets. Here he was, wrapping his thin legs around a branch of the *makopa* tree in the neighbor's backyard, stuffing his mouth with the unripe fruit until his belly ached. There he was in that sleepy, southern town, spending long afternoons watching the haze lift from the greenish water by the harbor pilings and smelling the sharp stench of the fires from the sugar cane fields, his mouth filled with the dust kicked up by the trucks as they lurched from pothole to pothole along the narrow streets.

There was not much for a young boy to do in the small town, other than play with the skinny dogs that lay heat-dazed in the middle of the street, only getting up reluctantly to avoid the occasional car. Mid-day, the dust steamed up from the streets and the sun glanced off the white-hot tin roofs, and everyone in town went to sleep and did not wake up again until the shadows were long across the plaza.

Nicanor, discovering all this, marveled. He wrote unceasingly for many days and nights. The childhood played at his feet, or threw balls of crumpled paper at him. He forgot to sleep or eat. He wrote in a trance. He did not notice when the childhood shrugged its shoulders and walked away, disappearing through an outer wall. He did not notice when something else entered the manuscript—an element of melancholy.

Beneath that powerful rush of remembered incidents and feelings was a strain of foreshadowing. The events seemed to be marching to one inevitable end.

Even as Nicanor wrote about the young Gomez playing in the tree-lined plaza fronting the old stone church, a secret voice whispered that the sun was setting and the shadows cast by the moss-grown walls of the church were creeping closer to where the boy tossed his marbles on the hard, packed earth. Soon, the voice whispered, the sun would set. Then, quickly, morning would come. And in this fashion, the voice whispered, the years would race by, the boy would grow up, and his hair would be speckled with white.

The fat wives of the *hacienda* owners who sat around in house dresses all day long, their hair in pin curlers, their soft, fleshy hands moving caressingly over the green and white mahjongg squares, did not hear the message, like a drum roll in the distant hills that seemed to accelerate with each passing day, hastening them to their deaths. The priest lecturing the dozing parishioners at Sunday Mass did not hear it. Neither did the man who sold *sorbetes* in the streets.

But Gomez heard it as he read, and the hearing filled him with apprehension and fear.

There were many in the town who provided abject lessons: The brave general's hair was now speckled with white. His brow sagged, his hair receded, his muscles grew slack and useless. He clutched at the *labandera* when she came to do the washing. The woman, Gomez's mother, felt his groping fingers, laughed and pushed him away, as though he were just another son who needed to be told to go out and play. Gomez's eyes were watchful, vigilant.

Years passed. There were no longer any books, for people had stopped reading when it became impossible to distinguish lies from the truth. People walked around in ignorance, and the villages were full of abandoned mansions where wild plants and weeds had invaded the silent rooms. The government news agencies and the Bureau of Censorship held the country in a grip so tight that if stories were still being written, they were being written in secret, behind sturdy doors in rooms without windows.

It seemed to Nicanor that the President had aged suddenly. His shoulders stooped. His mouth had a depressed look. The hair was not white, as Nicanor had envisioned it would be, but was a wispy grey, and very little of it remained.

These days when Nicanor let himself in at the service entrance to the Palace, he saw no one. The kitchen was strangely silent; the pots and pans hung untouched on the iron hooks. He walked alone down the empty, badly lit corridors. He wondered at the absence of people, and at the unfamiliar sound, which he later determined was the wind, howling around sharp corners. He wondered who could have left the windows open, and felt a momentary anxiety at the thought of the red billowy curtains blowing inward and knocking lamps off tables and books off shelves. Then he saw the bats, hanging upside down on the rafters. He hurried down the corridor, as if pursued by demons.

The President kept him waiting longer and longer. Once Nicanor fell asleep on the couch and when he opened his eyes, and saw he was still alone, he rose in a kind of panic. But almost in the next moment, the door at the far end of the room opened, and the President walked in slowly. Then they resumed the ritual reading of the manuscript, the ritual of the furrowed brow, the vaguely condescending handshake.

One day, the President simply sat and stared at the manuscript Nicanor placed in front of him. He looked down, but he was not reading. His eyes told Nicanor that the President was really very far away, that he was perhaps in the village of his childhood, feeling death.

As Nicanor left the Palace, he turned and looked at the balcony of the President's office. For a moment he remembered the times he used to watch the President making speeches, and then he realized the President had not stepped out for a very long time. He thought he caught a glimpse of an unfamiliar profile in the room, and felt an impulse to rush back. But he remained standing on the sidewalk, and after some moments a thin hand drew the red velvet curtains shut.

On his last visit to the Palace, the President came in, after a long wait, and sat heavily at his desk. He was very pale and Nicanor asked him if he wanted a drink of water. He smiled faintly but refused. He looked hard at Nicanor, almost as if he were seeing him for the first time.

"When did you lose your teeth?" he asked.

"About seven years ago," Nicanor replied. "I never bothered with dentures. I've lost my appetite and food doesn't appeal to me any longer."

The President nodded, as if in agreement. Then he reached for the papers Nicanor had placed on his desk. But he looked up, and seemed to struggle for a few moments.

"Did you see anyone—when you were coming in?" he asked Nicanor. "Any of the servants?"

"They are gone," Nicanor replied. After a few moments, he added, "I don't think it is coming back."

The President opened his mouth to laugh, and Nicanor saw that the teeth were broken and stumpy, like the teeth of a pig. The sight of this soundlessly laughing mouth so unnerved him that for the rest of the interview he kept his eyes stubbornly fastened on the floor. After a cursory glance at the manuscript the President dismissed him. But he did not get up to shake Nicanor's hand. He remained seated at the desk, his head between his hands.

That was the last time Nicanor ever saw him. From time to time, he heard about the promulgation of the latest edicts to issue from the palace. But such information ceased to interest him. He remained in the Archives, and if anyone had seen him, they might have mistaken him for a ghost; he was so thin and shrunken.

The President was no longer interested in his Special Research Project. He had a new obsession—to find the fabled treasure of General Yamashita, the commander of Japanese forces in the Philippines during World War II. It was rumored that the treasure was buried underneath the dungeons of Fort Santiago. The President hired foreign experts to conduct tests at the site, and they told him that underneath the dungeons there was so much water from an undisclosed source that it would take many years to pump it all out. Now the President had the pumps going night and day. Alone in his room at night, he muttered to himself. His aides sometimes heard words like "treasure" or "gold," or, sometimes, "pump." And these were repeated so often that they feared the President had lost his mind.

The President appointed a new Minister of Buildings and Construction. This man had never heard of the President's Special Research Project. A group of Japanese businessmen approached him with the idea of putting up a hotel on the site where the building that housed the National Archives stood. It was prime real estate, the businessmen pointed out, for which they were willing to pay unspecified millions of dollars.

"Gold," the minister said, as though he too had become infected with the Yamashita fever. He stroked his chin thoughtfully. He thought he could already imagine the crisp bills in his long fingers. He nodded.

They were ripping out the guts of the old building. They were hammering at the old walls. The walls were shuddering, collapsing in a cloud of dust, burying Nicanor's books and manuscripts. For days the city reverberated with the dull explosion of the wrecker's ball hitting unresisting walls and the furious drilling of jackhammers. When the noise finally ceased and the dust lifted, there was nothing left of the old building but a flattened pile of rubble.

No one thought to tell President Gomez about the ignominious end of his Special Research Project. He sat alone, neglected, in his Palace, listening to the strange sounds of destruction from across the river. At times he would be seized by a fit of violent trembling, like a victim of malarial fever. Then his eyes would flash, he would say angrily, "Let them come for me. I'm not afraid of them. I've always been ready for a fight." But no one came. If he listened carefully, he might hear the hard scrabble of rats' claws along the marble floors, or the cooing of birds nesting in the window eaves. But that was all. As far as everyone was concerned, he had long ago ceased to rule.

Island

Every summer they made the trip to Bacolod on one of the Negros Navigation boats, either the Don Juan or the Doña Florentina. The trip took nearly an entire day.

For a long time there was nothing to see out on the deck, only water stretching everywhere to the horizon. Cecilia and her sister would watch the furrows the boat's passing created in the water. She noted in particular the way the color of the water seemed to change, becoming very dark, still, and heavy-looking out beyond the reach of the boat's passing. Or, trying to scare each other, they would tell each other stories they had read about giant octopi and sharks and then keep watch for the dark bobbing shapes.

Cecilia was aware of how deep the ocean was, and she often imagined herself shipwrecked, trying to think how long she could tread water before becoming tired, before help would come.

Lately, Cecilia has been thinking more about those early childhood trips. The blue and grey water. The white clouds. The dolphins gamboling in the distance. They were essentials now. They offset the sterility of the white-coated doctors who probed at her belly and between her legs and told her strange words that to them seemed sufficient to explain why she could never have a child. Words like "endometriosis." The first mention of it was like some dread disease. But it was only some thing backed-up, building up inside, blocking passages that should not be blocked. "It's not malignant at all," the doctors said. "It's harmless. It could build up forever."

Then there were the other words: "ovarian cysts," "pelvic adhesions." Were the doctors actually talking about her? Cecilia looked down at the smooth skin on her belly in alarm. At night she spread her palms over her stomach and tried to feel these so-called adhesions, these bits of matter that were rotting away her tubes and her uterus and her organs and also, incidentally, her life.

There were times she thought she could feel the baby—or, anyway, the baby that would never come. Her stomach felt heavy. There was an ache near her belly button. Her thighs felt soft and tender. But the tests always came back negative. Then, as if that were the signal her body was waiting for, the menstrual blood would flow. It was heavier lately, heavier and clotted with membranes that she found herself looking over, as though to decipher some secret code.

Stop it, Cecilia finally told herself. Now, after work, after arriving home and kicking off her shoes, she and her husband were silent. She brought up the idea of going back to the Philippines, just for a visit. It had been twelve years.

She began to tell her husband stories: On the boat at night, the attendants partitioned the deck with canvas screens, and the passengers in second class stretched out on cots behind the screens. She liked to listen to the murmurs of these passengers in the darkness. Sometimes a lamp shone behind the canvas, and then she could make out dimly illuminated shadows—figures of people sitting up and going about their toilets. The night was black and cold, and the wind whipped her hair in all directions. The water down below was indescribably dark, and full of mystery.

She knew they were getting close to Bacolod when the islands appeared. The boat went in and out among these islands, sometimes quite close, but in all her trips she had never seen anyone standing by the shore. Sometimes, if they happened to pass the islands at night, she thought she could make out tiny lights, way up in the hills. She thought of woodcutters' huts and kerosene lamps. But for the most part the islands were very small, and very densely wooded. They, too, were full of secrets.

Their first sight of Bacolod was a barely distinguishable thin line against the horizon. After the land sighting, the trip seemed to come to an end very quickly. The boat surged powerfully, inexorably forward until it seemed only a matter of minutes before they could make out the palm trees, and then the piers. The water began to reflect numerous colors, and gave off a smell. Close to shore it was more brown than blue. When the boat had ground against the pier and been made fast, there was no more time to think. Everyone was busy getting their bags together and shouting down to the people on the pier below. They squeezed down the narrow wooden gangplank, trying to keep their shoes from getting muddy and from being stepped on. It seemed there was always a man there waiting to grab their bags, someone who knew their parents, who spoke to their mother and father in familiar tones as if they were old friends, but whom the children did not recognize. This man would carry their bags to a waiting car idling with the air conditioner running. He inevitably had bony arms and legs, and skin the color of dark polished wood. He never looked at the children, but steered them expertly to where they needed to go. Cecilia always felt uncomfortable in the presence of this stranger, not knowing what to say to make the pain of having to carry her bags any easier, but her parents talked easily, asking about the weather and the crops and other inconsequential matters, as if the man were not actually carrying their luggage, as if this carrying of bags were such a natural thing that it could easily be ignored.

They would get into the car and the stranger would slip into the driver's seat and, although she could not remember her mother or father telling him where to go, he seemed to go in the direction that satisfied them, as if directed by unseen radar. They passed stands of coconut trees and low one-story buildings. She always remembered the ice plant, because immediately after that came the city. It was not a city like Manila, because it was not crowded, and there were not many buildings. It was called Bacolod City, and there were a few department stores, a tree-lined plaza, and a very nice hotel overlooking the bay.

They were driven to the Big House, which was what everybody called the three-story building on Burgos Street, the one with the red iron gates. There was a statue of a German Shepherd, head raised and ears cocked as if listening to something, at the foot of the driveway. There was a pond, filled with stagnant green water, and a multitude of darting black shapes that she and her sister liked to scoop out in little glass jars. They saw the big mongrels, and the people, many people. Some were aunts and uncles and cousins. Others lived in the low building behind the Big House, and were so mysterious she could not explain exactly why she felt shy in their presence. She knew they were the mothers and fathers of the little barefoot boys she saw running about, and when she and her sister approached and tried to be friendly, the boys invariably giggled, with their hands before their mouths. She saw them very rarely in the upstairs rooms, and then only in the mornings, when they cleaned.

"What a decadent life," Cecilia's husband liked to say.

"Was it, really?" she would find herself asking, surprised. She did not know why she had begun to tell the stories. But once she had begun, she didn't want to stop.

After a week or two, Cecilia told her husband, her parents left for Manila, leaving her and her sister in the care of their aunts and uncles. The girls did not miss their parents, because in that house was a room filled with boxes of DC comics. There must have been at least twenty boxes of them—comics that had once belonged to cousins, and never been thrown away. There was also another room, a room that belonged to a spinster aunt, with a whole wall lined with Mills & Boon paperbacks. Oh, it was heaven to read such trash for days on end, stopping only when called to eat. In Manila, their mother had strict rules about reading matter, but in Bacolod she seemed to think whatever her children read was all right, perhaps because she equated summer in Bacolod with not thinking. Perhaps.

Oh, and the food! Mountains of it: sweet sugary sausage, crumbled up and fried until almost black; sticky *kalamayhati* from coconut shells; *empanadas* from the baskets of the women who came by every afternoon at four o'clock; *barkilyos* from the big tin labeled *Panaderias de molo*. There were crab eggs and fish roe—heaven to eat on rice sprinkled with lemon juice. And *tinapa* for breakfast, and *karne norte* with eggs.

Cecilia could have gone on and on, only she would notice that her husband seemed bored. He wanted to read a newspaper, to listen to the latest sports results on the TV. Perhaps she was getting a little carried away by this food business. Again she had to think: I never talked like this until I began to see the doctors.

It was not only the food. It was the actual smell of the place she could remember—the smells emanating from the two mongrel dogs that seemed perpetual fixtures under the dining room table. The smells emanating from the kitchen, a pungent smell as of blood and innards, mixed with other, homelier smells, smells of sour milk, of fried fish. She could remember, too, the flies that hovered around the food and were swished away by maids with large *abaká* fans. They were twice the size of flies she saw here, with glossy blue-green wings on which she could clearly see a tracery of membranes. It amazed her to think how much she actually retained from those years and how long she had forgotten them.

Waking up some mornings, Cecilia felt an ache in the pit of her belly. This ache was so real that she would find herself throwing up in the kitchen sink. Then it seemed to her that her hands and feet were beginning to swell. She knew the feeling, having been pregnant once before, a long time ago. That baby had been lost. But she had carried it long enough to know the weight of it inside her, and to feel sharp, probing movements. Now there were times when she thought she could feel that baby once again.

At night she dreamed she was holding a little oval cotton blanket in her arms. It smelled of *Nenuco* and Johnson's Baby Powder. In her dream she felt a sense of accomplishment and wonder. She felt at peace, the warmth pressed against her chest. Be careful, be careful, she found herself whispering. Tenderly she patted the little shape. How light it seemed.

"You're making things up," Cecilia's husband told her. "I don't believe things were ever that idyllic there. You were probably bored most of the time."

Not true, not true! In Bacolod she was a different person—heavier and dark, her back and arms patterned with the outlines of her swimsuit. She did not cry when she skinned her knees climbing the mango trees. She did not run from the thunder that sounded so close here. She did not flinch when the houseboys brought her lizards tethered on strings.

Her aunts took her to a resort. To get to the kiddie pool, you had to pass underneath a pavilion, through a tunnel whose stone walls breathed dampness and moss. She walked the tunnel fearlessly, imagining herself an Amazon warrior. The floor was not simply wet but slippery—as though something thicker, more viscous than water, had collected there between the large stones. Her bare feet stepped confidently, her toes firmly gripping the slippery paving stones.

At one end of the pool was a stone elephant painted white, rearing its trunk into the air. Fearlessly she climbed on this elephant's back. His back felt hard and hot, and she could see the paint chipping and the grey stone coming out in patches all over. The thick, unevenly applied paint felt grainy beneath her thighs. She felt the hot sun on her back, on her shoulders. She lay stomach down over the elephant's back, the conquering Amazon queen.

"I nearly died there once," Cecilia told her husband. "I was only five. I was with my *yaya* but she wasn't paying attention to me and I wandered out to the deep part of the pool and nearly drowned. A nun jumped into the water and rescued me. She had a long black habit and a white veil. She jumped in, fully clothed, and waded out to me."

Her husband looks as though he does not believe her. But she can remember the feeling of the water entering her nose and throat, and how strange the world had looked from under a few feet of water—all bright lights and darting shapes, with nothing distinguishable. She remembers now why the *yaya* had not come: there was a young lifeguard who worked there, and the *yaya* was always wandering over to talk to him. Perhaps they had even wandered off together for a few moments. She didn't actually remember the part about the nun. It was her mother who told her. "She jumped into the water, clothes and all!" her mother exclaimed. Now, years later, Cecilia imagines this nun moving slowly toward her five-year-old self, moving in a waterlogged black habit that spreads out on the water like the hood of a jellyfish. She imagines what followed later: "I was so angry," her mother says. "I sent your *yaya* away. I didn't even wait for her to pack her things. I threw them out the door. And there you were," her mother says, laughing and wiping a tear from her eye, "crying and hanging on to your *yaya*'s legs as though we had beaten you. We had to get your father to pry you loose. It was the craziest thing."

Cecilia's husband makes a faint movement. He is sitting on the sofa by the brass standing lamp, and the light throws into relief the lines on his face, lines she had not noticed before. There is gray around his temples, and his skin, she sees now, is scarred and pitted. His eyes are watchful and reserved, but she doesn't ask what he is thinking. Instead, she goes over to him and holds his hand. It is a bony hand, with long fingers, and they curl around hers now. They are both silent for a few moments.

"You weren't afraid," he says now, "afraid of the water? Afraid you might drown?"

"No. Strangely, I wasn't. I always knew someone would come and help me."

She is more afraid now, though she has not told anyone, not even her husband. The fear comes when she thinks about the future, and of her husband and herself growing old without children. In the fairy tales she remembers from her childhood, there was always some wicked witch who was telling the good people, usually a king and queen, "You will not be able to bear a child," or, "I shall take your child away from you." There were always such dangers surrounding the children, those precious beings. They got lost in the woods. They fell down deep wells. They fell into deep sleep and were surrounded by forests of thorns. Then it would take someone in shining armor hacking away at the forest, and even he needed a magic charm to prevail. Where is our magic charm, she wonders now?

She fears extinction. Perhaps this is the wrong reason to want a child. It wasn't the reason, in the beginning. But it has become the reason, lately. Without knowing why, she begins to cry. She tries to hide it from her husband, but—

"It's okay," he says softly, and she feels the pressure of his fingers. "It's okay. Tell me more about Bacolod."

Cecilia stops and wipes her face with the back of her hand. She searches her memory for the one shining thing. She tells him: "I had a playmate once. Her name was Ning-ning. Did I ever tell you that she wrote to me? It was a long time ago, and I never wrote her back. Her mother was ill. Her mother was so sick. Oh, I should have written her back, but I didn't know how I could help. You were out of a job then. It was hard."

She thinks about Ning-ning, about their last meeting. They were both eighteen years old. Ning-ning was still so small, as small as Cecilia was when she was twelve. She wore her hair cut short, like a boy's. She held a tray of beer bottles, and she was heading toward one of the resort cottages.

"Ning-ning, I am going away, I am going to America!" Cecilia told her. Ning-ning stopped and looked at her. What she saw on Ning-ning's face was a new guardedness. It troubled her.

"Oh, Ning-ning," she said. "What is wrong? What is it?"

Ning-ning turned her face away. She shook her head stubbornly. The beer bottles slid precariously on the tray. "Who is that for?" she asked Ning-ning, and at this Ning-ning looked up defiantly and laughed. "An old lady in one of the cottages—a sugar mommy. You should see the boy she picked up! Younger than me, even."

Cecilia felt faint. She took Ning-ning's hand. It was soft and limp. "Oh," she began, "I won't forget you. I'll ask my father if he can't find a better job for you somewhere."

Ning-ning looked grateful. She said, "Tell him I'm the daughter of Ramona. He may not remember. But my mother took care of his father when his father had become a paralytic, when he had to be carried everywhere. Tell him!"

"I will," she said. It occurred to her that she had some money, and impulsively she dug into her pockets and fished out all she had: a few crumpled *pesos,* a handful of coins. She thrust these into the pockets of Ning-ning's dress, even though Ning-ning tried to pull away. She was embarrassed, but she also needed to accept the money.

"I won't forget to tell my father," she said to Ning-ning.

But, driving back to Bacolod City from the resort, she had already forgotten her promise. It was a hot day, and the coconut palms that lined the highway were listless. Their crowns seemed to droop. She looked around her at the fields of sugar cane, the signs marking where one hacienda ended and another began: Hacienda Patricia, Hacienda Luisita. Familiar names, names from her family's past. She was sad at the thought of leaving, but excited, too, at the thought of America. That night there was a party, and everyone drank to her good fortune. She never told her father about her promise to Ning-ning.

Cecilia jumps up from the sofa, and releases her husband's hand. "Oh, God!" she says. "I have to write her this minute!"

The memory tears at her emotionally, just as the thought of what is not in her belly tears at her physically. She clutches her stomach now. The pain is really too much. She sees her husband as a dim shape, still seated on the sofa, his features indistinguishable.

Glossary

abaká Hemp.

ale There is no English equivalent for this expression. It can be used variously to mean "Ma'am," "Madam," or "Auntie." Generally used as a conventional title of courtesy when the speaker does not know the name of the woman being addressed.

aling A conventional title of courtesy, more familiar than *ale*, used before the first name of the woman being addressed.

Aman Namin Our Father. The first words of the Lord's Prayer in Tagalog.

Americana A European-style coat.

anting-anting Amulet, magic charm.

ate Sister.

Bahala na Leave it to fate.

balut Boiled duck's egg with partially developed embryo (a native delicacy).

bancas A long, slender canoe-like boat.

barkilyos Thin sweet wafers, usually in cylindrical rolls, a native dessert.

Bawal Umihi Dito Sign frequently seen on Manila streets. (Literal translation: Urinating Prohibited Here.)

bolo Long, curved knife.

camias Native flower, used in making medicinal preparation for "nerves."

carabao Water buffalo.

chismis The fine art of Filipino gossip.

colegiala Female college student.

El Señor The Master (ironic usage—not a literal translation).

empanada Crescent-shaped, meat-filled pastry, usually deep-fried.

enkargado A caretaker, a foreman.

galunggong Fish resembling scad; staple of the poor Filipinos' diet.

gumamela Hibiscus.

herbolario Person who practices folk medicine, often by dispensing medicinal herbs.

iha "Daughter." An appellation by an elder addressing a young girl for whom he feels fondness.

huramentado Adjective, rough equivalent of "running amok;" or, as a noun, "person who runs amok."

Ina Mother.

Kalamansi Small, native lime.

kalamayhati Sweet conserve made from coconut milk and brown sugar, often sold in a container made from a coconut shell.

kamatis Tomato.

karne norte Corned beef.

Kumusta ka How are you?

labandera Washerwoman.

lanai Open porch/terrace.

makopa A tree, about 10 m. high, with small, tart red fruit.

Mamang Mother.

Mang A term of respect when referring to elderly men, used before the first name.

Maria Makiling A mythical character, frequently mentioned in Filipino legends. She was a very beautiful woman who lived on a mountain and often gave gifts to the poor.

masa The mass of people, the multitude.

merienda A snack, usually between lunch and supper.

mestiza Woman of mixed descent (usually, Spanish and Filipino).

Nang From the Visayan dialect, a word with roughly the same meaning as *Aling*.

narra Philippine hardwood, now rare.

nipa Thatch made of dried coconut palm leaves.

nobyo/nobya Boyfriend/girlfriend.

padrón A benefactor.

Pampangueño A native of Pampanga (a province in the Philippines).

Panaderías de Molo Label found on cookie tins from Molo, a small town in Negros province famous for its bakeries.

pandesal Sweet bread buns.

pare Form of address to a male familiar. Sometimes used when the speaker does not know the name of the person being addressed and wishes to be polite.

peso Philippine paper currency.

piyaya Philippine delicacy made with unleavened dough and caramelized sugar (native to the region south of Manila known as the Visayas).

pomada A type of hair oil.

puta Prostitute.

rebelde A rebel. Also used as an adjective to mean "rebellious."

sakadas Seasonal laborers. A term used in the Visayas, the sugar-growing region of the Philippines, to refer to laborers brought in from other districts or islands for the duration of the harvest and milling season.

santan Flower native to the Philippines.

santol Philippine fruit.

sari-sari An assortment (As in *"sari-sari* store"—the neighborhood grocery store).

sibuyas Onions.

singkit Small and almond-shaped, in referring to eyes.

sorbetes Sherbert.

stupida Stupid.

suwerte Luck, to be lucky.

taho Chinese dessert: soybeans in sweet syrup. Sold as a drink by street peddlers.

talahib A species of wild grass: tall, tufted, with coarse leaves. Usually found in open lands or, in the city, in vacant lots.

tamaraw A small wild buffalo, renowned for fierceness, native to the Philippines.

Tatang Father.

taya "It," a child's game.

tikbalang Folkloric creature whose supposed pastime is to get people to lose their way. He looks like an ordinary person except for certain telltale signs, which may vary according to the storyteller: sometimes he is said to have horses' feet, at other times the area between the nose and mouth is said to be smooth, like a monkey's.

tinapa Smoked fish.

tsampoy Chinese fruit snack, made from dried berries.

titina Salty snack sold in Chinese groceries in Manila

tiyanggi A store.

tsinelas Slippers.

tuba Native drink made from fermented palm sap.

turo-turos Philippine fastfood eatery: a small restaurant where the food is served cafeteria-style.

Walang hiya ka Curse, roughly translated as "How shameless you are!"

yaya Nursemaid, governess.

zarzuela A musical play, popular during the Spanish colonial period.

NOTE: The Tagalog language contains many words derived from Spanish. Tagalog spelling differs slightly from the Spanish, though in many cases the meaning is the same in both languages.

About the Author

Marianne Villanueva is the Project Coordinator for the Stanford East Asia National Resource Center (SEANRC).She received her B.A. from Ateneo University, Manilla (Philippines) and MA's in Creative Writing and East Asian Studies from Stanford University (CA).

She has been published in *Matrix, The Forbidden Stitch: An Asian American Women's Anthology* (Calyx Books, 1989), *Story Quarterly, Panorama* (Sunday magazine of the *Manila Bulletin*), *Journal of Philippine Studies, Asiaweek,* and *Filipinas Journal.*

She won a 1990 *New Letters* award from the University of Missouri, Kansas City, and was also a finalist for the Joseph Henry Jackson Memorial Award. She was twice the winner of the Ateneo de Manila Playwriting Contest in the English Division, and in 1976 was a National Fellow at the University of the Philippines' Writers'Workshop.

Virginia R. Cerenio is a second-generation Filipina-American. Her poems and short stories have appeared in numerous publications, including *Breaking Silence* (Greenfield Review Press), *Without Names* (Kearny Street Workshop Press), *Berkeley Fiction Review* (U.C. Berkeley), *Asian Journal* (Columbia University), and *Liwanaq*. Her collection of poetry, *Trespassing Innocence,* was published in 1989 by Kearny Street Workshop Press.

Colophon

*The text of this book was composed in Stone Serif
with Stone Sans Serif initial capitals.
Typeset by ImPrint Services, Corvallis, Oregon.*

Selected Award-Winning Titles from CALYX Books

Idleness Is the Root of All Love, by Christa Reinig, translated from the German by Ilze Mueller. Tender and angry love poems documenting two older lesbians' year together.
ISBN 0-934971-21-8, $10, paper; ISBN 0-934971-22-6, $18.95, cloth.

The Forbidden Stitch: An Asian American Women's Anthology, edited by Shirley Geok-lin Lim, et. al. The first Asian American women's anthology. Winner of the American Book Award.
ISBN 0-934971-04-8, $16.95, paper; ISBN 0-934971-10-2, $29.95, cloth.

Women and Aging, An Anthology by Women, edited by Jo Alexander, et. al. The only anthology that addresses ageism from a feminist perspective.
ISBN 0-934971-00-5, $15.95, paper; ISBN 0-934971-07-2, $28.95, cloth.

In China with Harpo and Karl, by Sibyl James. Essays revealing a feminist poet's experiences while teaching in Shanghai, PRC.
ISBN 0-934971-15-3, $9.95, paper; ISBN 0-934971-16-1, $17.95, cloth.

Indian Singing in 20th Century America, by Gail Tremblay. A work of hope by a Native American poet.
ISBN 0-934971-13-7, $8.95, paper; ISBN 0-934971-14-5, $16.95, cloth.

The Riverhouse Stories, by Andrea Carlisle. A classic! Unlike any other lesbian novel published.
ISBN 0-934971-01-3, $8.95, paper; ISBN 0-934971-08-0, $16.95, cloth.

CALYX Books is committed to producing books of literary, social, and feminist integrity.

CALYX Books are available in your local bookstore, or direct from:

CALYX Books, P.O. Box B, Corvallis, OR 97339

(Please include payment with your order. Add $1.50 postage for first book and $.75 for each additional book.)

CALYX, Inc., is a nonprofit organization
with a 501(C)(3) status.
All donations are tax deductible.